THE GUNSMITH

#414 DEATH OF A GANDY DANCER

PRO SE ⚖ PRESS

THE GUNSMITH #414: DEATH OF A GANDY DANCER
A Pro Se Press Publication

THE GUNSMITH #414: DEATH OF A GANDY DANCER is a work of historical fiction. Many of the important historical events, figures, and locations are as accurately portrayed as possible. In keeping with a work of fiction, various events and occurrences were invented by the author.

Edited by Tommy Hancock and Kristi King-Morgan
Editor in Chief, Pro Se Productions—Tommy Hancock
Submissions Editor—Rachel Lampi
Director of Corporate Operations—Kristi King-Morgan
Publisher & Pro Se Productions, LLC-Chief Executive Officer—Fuller Bumpers

Cover Art by Jeffrey Hayes
Print Production and Book Design by Percival Constantine
New Pulp Logo Design by Sean E. Ali
New Pulp Seal Design by Cari Reese

Pro Se Productions, LLC
133 1/2 Broad Street
Batesville, AR, 72501
870-834-4022

editorinchief@prose-press.com
www.prose-press.com

THE GUNSMITH #414: DEATH OF A GANDY DANCER

Published in digital form by Piccadilly Publishing,

THE GUNSMITH

#414 DEATH OF A GANDY DANCER

J.R. ROBERTS

PROSE PRESS

ONE

Clint Adams could smell the lumber camp before he reached it.

Oregon had miles and miles of trees—cedar, hemlock, pine, spruce—all waiting to be cut down and used to build wagons, homes and towns.

The men who cut down these trees were a special breed, with very particular talents. Clint had received a telegram from one such man, a friend of his named Tom Allen. Usually, when a telegram found its way to him in Labyrinth, Tx, it meant some kind of trouble, and Rick Hartman knew it...

***

He was in Rick's Saloon when the telegraph key operator came in and handed him the telegram.

"Oh, great," Rick said, from behind the bar where he was playing temporary bartender until he could hire a new one. "Who's in trouble this time?"

Clint unfolded the telegram, read it and said with relief, "Nobody."

"You mean it's good news?" Rick asked. "That's a switch."

"Tom Allen."

Rock frowned, then brightened. "The lumber guy?"

1

"That's him," Clint said. "He's in Oregon."

Rick leaned on the bar.

"Lots of lumber there. He need help cuttin' it down?"

"No," Clint said, "he says he's competing for a contract and why don't I come up and watch."

"Watch what?"

"A competition for the contract," Clint said. "He's going to compete against other loggers, and the one who wins gets the contract."

"So he doesn't want help," Rick said, "he wants an audience?"

"Maybe just some moral support," Clint said, folding the telegram and putting it into his pocket.

"So, you gonna go?"

"I am," Clint said. "It sounds interesting, and it's all about trees, not guns."

"When are you leavin'?"

"Tomorrow morning."

"Then here," Rick said, sliding a mug over to him, "have another beer... on the house."

"Thanks."

"And while you're there, do me a favor."

"What's that?"

"Don't let any trees fall on you."

***

Most of the trip was done by rail, but Clint preferred to ride into Oregon on Eclipse's back, and he still had several days before the lumberjack contest Tom Allen had mentioned was to begin.

Now, as he followed the scent of freshly cut wood, he was expecting to see a lumber camp. Instead, as he came over a hill and broke from a clump of pine trees,

2

he saw a town.

He hadn't been to Oregon in some time, and never to this part. Still, he hadn't expected to find a town. When he reached it, though, he discovered the reason. All the buildings were brand new. This place had sprung up practically overnight, and the smell of fresh lumber hung over it like a cloud.

Tom Allen had told Clint to meet him in Jackson County. That's where the job, and the competition, was going to be. As he rode Eclipse down the main street of the town he still didn't know the name of, he saw a hotel, two saloons, a general store, pretty much everything needed... except for a bank.

He reined in Eclipse in front of one of the saloons, dropped his reins to the ground, and stepped up onto the boardwalk. The town seemed to be so new that it either didn't have a name yet, or just hadn't put up any signs.

As he went through the batwing doors, the eight or ten men drinking inside turned to look at him. He didn't find it odd that in lumber country, only two of them were wearing guns. The others were all lumberjacks.

He approached the bar under their watchful eyes.

"Beer," he told the bartender.

"That depends," the middle-aged man said.

"On what?" Clint asked. "Don't you have beer?"

"Yeah, we got beer," the man said.

"So, I'll have one."

"We don't serve it to just anybody," the bartender said.

"Then it's lucky I'm nobody," Clint said. "I just rode into town and I want a cold beer."

The bartender looked to his left, and Clint heard several chairs scrape the floor. He looked that way, saw three unarmed lumberjacks walking towards him.

"Well now," one of them said, "it's still gonna depend."

"On what?" Clint asked.

"On who you are," the man said, "and who you're here to see."

All three men were well over six feet tall, and brawny. In a fight with them he wouldn't stand a chance. Fortunately, he had no intention of fighting.

"My name's Clint Adams," he said, "and I'm here to see Tom Allen."

The men stared at him and said nothing, but from the back another voice boomed out, "You're Tommy's friend?"

Clint looked past the three men to an even larger man who was advancing toward him with a big grin on his face. He brushed past the three men, grabbed Clint in a bear hug and lifted him off the floor.

"Give this man a beer!" he bellowed.

TWO

The huge man swung Clint around in a hug and then set him back on the floor.

"You guys go back to your drinkin'," he told the three men. "And you, Blackie, two beers. Come on," he said to the bartender.

"Comin' up, Luke."

The big man turned to Clint and put out his hand.

"Luke Connors," he said. "Some folks around here call me Big Luke."

"Clint," Clint said, shaking hands.

Blackie the bartender put two huge glasses of beer on the bar.

"Drink up," Luke said. "You need it if you just rode in.

"You got that right." Clint took a healthy swig. "So, is Tom around?"

"He's around, just not in town, right now," Luke said.

"Does this place have a name?"

"I's a work in progress," Luke said.

"You sound pretty educated for a lumberjack," Clint said.

"What? You think we're all morons?"

"I never said that."

Luke drank down half of his beer and said, "I always get that." he put his mug down on the bar. "I was educated

5

back East." He held up two fingers. "Two degrees."

"In what?"

"I don't remember," Luke said. "I need fresh air and wide open spaces, and here I am."

"How long have you been up here cutting down trees?"

"Ten years."

"Tom's been here what? Two?"

"That's right."

"Has he been working with you that whole time?"

"More like I've been working with him," Luke said. "The man knows what he's doing."

"So then you know about this competition he sent me a telegram about?"

"Everybody around here knows about that," Luke said. "The job is cutting down the trees on the Boyce property."

"Boyce?"

"Harry Boyce," Luke said. "He owns the biggest spread up here."

"What kind of spread?"

"Everything," Luke said. "Horses, cattle... and trees."

"How many men are competing for the job?"

"Not sure," Luke said, "but it's got to be over twenty."

"What about you?"

"I'm in there," Luke said, "but if I win, the job goes to Tom, because I work for him."

"Is anybody else competing for Tom?"

"No, just him and me. Unless that's why you're here?"

"Me? A lumberjack?" Clint asked. "Not a chance. I'm here for moral support."

"Well," Luke said, "we could use a little more than that."

6

"What do you mean?"

Luke finished his beer and pushed the empty mug away.

"Seems like somebody's trying to hedge their bets."

"How so?"

"Well, there's been two close calls for Tom," Luke said. "A branch fell from a tree and just missed him, and a runaway buckboard almost ran him down."

"Both deliberate?"

"We think so."

"Any ideas as to who might've done it?"

"If there's twenty competitors," Luke said, "there's eighteen suspects."

Clint finished his beer and pushed his empty mug say to join Luke's.

"So tell me why I got the reception I got when I asked for a beer," he said.

"There's some fellas in here who don't like strangers," Luke said, "and there's lots of fellas who don't like anybody who works for Boyce."

"Is Boyce the typical big rancher?" Clint asked.

"Let's put it this way," Luke said. "He wants to call this town Boyce."

"Oh yeah," Clint said, "he's a typical arrogant, rich rancher, then."

"Tom will have a lot more to tell you," Luke said.

"What's he doing out there?"

"He's out looking over the job."

"So he's on the Boyce property, now?" Clint asked.

"He is."

"Alone?"

"Yep."

Clint shook his head.

"Can you take me out there?" Clint asked. "He

shouldn't be alone."

Luke shook his head.

"There's a lot of miles out there," he said, "we'd never find him. You'd be better off waiting for him to get back and then giving him a piece of your mind."

"Oh, I'll do that, all right," Clint said. "If there's been two close calls already, then he's being foolish going out there by himself."

"Well, Tom Allen doesn't scare," Luke said. "If you know him, you know that."

"I do," Clint said, "and I also know it could end up getting him killed."

"We're thinking alike, then," Luke said. "Let's have another beer on it."

"Sounds good to me."

THREE

Luke walked Clint down the street.

"This is our only hotel," the big man said. "Tom got you a room here, so you're already registered."

"And my horse?"

"There's a livery just up the street and around the corner," Luke said. "I can take him over, if you like."

"No," Clint said, "I'll take care of him myself. You must have other things to do."

"Yeah," Luke said, "I've got to get my axe sharpened."

"Yeah, right," Clint said, smiling.

"No," Luke said, "I'm serious."

"Oh."

"Tom will be back in a couple of hours," Luke said. "You want to eat something while you wait?"

"I'm kind of hungry."

"Right over there," Luke said, pointing, "is a small café. The food's pretty good, unless you want a nice thick steak."

"That can come later," Clint said. "I just need a little something."

"That's the place, then."

"Okay," Clint said. "I'll get my horse situated, get my room, and have something to eat."

"Maybe Tom will be back by then."

"If not, he can find me in the saloon or my room when he gets back."

"Go to the same saloon," Luke said. "Some of the men in the other one won't like that you're here for Tom."

"Okay, I've got it."

"I'll see you later."

Clint started walking toward the livery and called back, "Get that blade nice and sharp!"

***

Clint came back from the livery with his rifle and saddlebags.

"Clint Adams," he told the young clerk. "I understand you have a room for me."

"Yes, sir." The clerk grabbed a key from the board behind him. "Number seven. Just up the stairs and down the hall."

"Thanks."

Clint went up to the second floor and entered room 7. The walls were bare, the room was clean, everything in it was new. He dropped the saddlebags onto the bed, leaned the rifle against the wall in a corner, and left.

"If anybody's looking for me I'll be in the café across the street."

"Yes, sir."

Clint left the hotel and walked to the café. There were a few people on the street, most of them men who looked like loggers. The few women looked him over as he went past them. All the people seemed to be walking intently with someplace to go, rather than just strolling. And the thing he noticed most was that none of them seemed to be over fifty.

He entered the café, saw that it held about ten tables,

and only a couple were taken.

"Sit anywhere you like," the waiter told him. "In the window?"

"No, thanks," Clint said, "a back table will do."

"Suit yourself."

Clint walked to the back and sat.

"What can I get you?" the waiter asked.

"Something quick," Clint said. "A sandwich?"

"Chicken all right?"

"That's fine. And some coffee—strong."

"Yes, sir." The waiter grinned broadly. He was the only person Clint had seen so far who might have been older than fifty.

The three people in the place were a man in his thirties, seated alone, not wearing a gun, and a man and a woman in their twenties, who were staring at each other like a couple would. They hadn't even looked at Clint when he entered.

The coffee came first, then the sandwich.

"Anything else?"

"No, this is fine. Thanks."

The chicken was white meat, cut up with onions in it, and the bread was very fresh. It was just what Clint needed to take the edge off after riding all morning. His breakfast had been just coffee, supper the night before just coffee and beef jerky. He hadn't had a good meal in two days.

***

When Tom Allen got to the saloon, Luke Connors was standing at the bar.

"That's just where you were when I left!" he bellowed, slapping Luke on the back and waving to the other men in the saloon. "Blackie, a beer."

"Comin' up."

"About time you got back," Luke said.

Allen accepted the beer from the bartender and drank down half of it. Luke was half a head larger than most of the men in town, but only a few inches taller than Tom Allen.

"What, you missed me?"

"No, but you missed your friend."

"Friend?" He drank some more beer, then got it. He looked at Luke. "Clint's here?"

"Yeah, he's at the hotel. Unless he's in the café."

"The café? He's not gonna get a steak there."

"He just wanted something until you got back."

"Well, I'm back. Let's go see him."

"Might as well try the café first," Luke said, as they headed for the door. "Then the hotel."

"I'm glad he finally made it," Allen said. "Now maybe things'll change."

FOUR

Clint put the last bite of sandwich into his mouth as Tom and Luke came through the door. The other diners had since left, and the place was empty.

"Clint!"

"Hey, Tom!"

He stood and the two men embraced. Tom Allen squeezed him almost as hard as Luke had, in his bear hug.

"Jesus," he said, "between the two of you I bet you broke a couple of my ribs."

"Ah," Tom, said, releasing him and slapping him on the shoulder, "you're made of sterner stuff than that." He looked at the table. "You done eatin'?"

"Just going to finish my coffee."

"Okay, we'll join you." Tom turned to look for the waiter. "We need more coffee!"

"Comin' up," the man called, from the kitchen. He appeared with another pot, and two more mugs. He poured for the three of them.

"Anythin' else?" he asked.

"Naw, that's it," Tom said. "Thanks."

"Sure thing."

Luke sat across from Clint, Tom to his left. On the right was the wall.

"I'm so glad you're here," Tom said.

"Your telegram said I'd have fun," Clint said.

"And you will."

"But Luke makes it sound like you need me for more than that. Like keeping you alive."

"I didn't know that when I sent the telegram."

"He told me about the accidents that might not have been accidents."

"Yeah, those things," Tom said, "they happened after I sent the telegram."

"So you think somebody's trying to kill you?"

"Maybe not kill," Tom said, "maybe just tryin' to keep me out of the competition."

"Then why would you go out to Boyce's ranch, alone?" Clint asked.

"I'm not gonna let them influence me," Tom said. "I'm not scared, Clint."

"Maybe you should be," Clint said. "Okay, look, now that I'm here, you're going to have to tell me everything."

"I can do that," Tom said, "but you need a bath, I need a bath..." He looked at Luke.

"I don't need a bath."

"You always need a bath," Tom said. He looked back at Clint. "We'll talk later, over supper. How does that sound?"

"So you're not going to leave town again?"

"No."

"I'll stay with him," Luke said.

"Okay," Clint said. "We'll talk later, and you'll have to show me where this competition is going to take place."

"Ah," Tom said, his eyes bright, "that's being put together even as we speak. Some of it's gonna be down by the river. But yeah, okay, later." He clapped his hands together. "I've been out among the trees all day. A bath!"

"Where?"

"You're in the hotel, right?"

"Right."

"Okay, so am I. They have bathtubs."

"I don't need a bath," Luke said, again. "But I could use another beer."

"You go ahead," Tom said. "Me and Clint will get cleaned up, and we'll meet you at the saloon. And then... steaks."

"Sounds good to me," Luke said.

Tom insisted on paying for Clint's sandwich, and then the three men left the café. Out front they split up, Luke going back to the saloon, while Clint and Tom walked to the hotel.

In the lobby, Tom called to the desk clerk, "Terry, get two hot baths ready, will you?"

"Sure thing, Mr. Allen."

"You wanna get some fresh clothes and meet me at the tubs?" Tom asked.

"I've got a fresh shirt."

"That's what I meant," Tom said.

As it turned out, they were on the same floor, Tom down the hall in room 11. They ended up going back down to the lobby together, and then down a hall to the room with four bathtubs, two of which were steaming. The clerk was there waiting.

"Here are your towels," he said. "Let me know if you need anything else."

"A chair," Clint said.

"What?"

"I need a chair here next to the tub."

The clerk looked confused, but said, "All right. Coming up."

He ran out and came back with a wooden chair,

which he set by the tub.

"Okay, thanks," Clint said. "That's good."

The clerk nodded and left.

Clint unstrapped his gun and hung it on the back of the chair.

"Oh," Tom said, "I wondered."

They undressed and each got into a tub with a groan.

"Wow, I needed this," Clint said.

"You made good time," Tom said.

"Mostly by rail, but there was still a lot of time in the saddle," Clint said.

"I appreciate you comin' all this way, Clint," Tom said.

"Well, I did it because this lumberjack competition sounded interesting," Clint said, "but now it seems like I'm here to keep you alive."

"Yeah," Tom said, "sorry about that. It was just supposed to be all fun and games."

"Well," Clint said, "why don't we see what we can do to keep it that way?"

FIVE

Clint and Tom entered the saloon, both clean and re-freshed and wearing a clean shirt. Tom waved to the other men, and they joined Luke at the bar, where he was finishing up a beer.

"Just in time," he said. "I was about to have another."

"Forget it," Tom said. "Time for those steaks. You can have a beer there."

"Works for me," Luke said. "Let's go."

They left the saloon and walked several blocks until Tom Allen stopped in front of a large building.

"You know how a lot of towns have a Cattleman's Club?" he asked.

"Is that what this is?"

"Almost," Tom said. "As soon as we get a sign made, this is gonna say 'The Lumberjack's Club.' Let's go inside."

Inside was large, and mostly empty except for tables and chairs.

"We're still working on getting some wooden chandeliers, and more furniture, but what we do have is a great cook."

"Mr. Allen," a man said, approaching them. He was in his forties, looked as if he'd be at home in a suit, but instead was dressed rustically, in jeans and a plaid shirt. "Big Luke. Welcome."

"Hey, Danny," Tom said. "Meet my friend Clint Adams."

"Mr. Adams, welcome."

"Thanks."

"We're gonna have three of Randy's biggest steaks," Tom said.

"Yessir. Take your usual table and I'll bring out three mugs of cold beer."

"Attaboy, Danny!" Luke cheered.

Tom led them to a round table near the back of the room that would have easily seated eight people.

"He looks so uncomfortable in that shirt and jeans," Clint said.

"I know," Tom said. "We grabbed him from a place in Kansas City where he used to wear a suit and tie all the time."

"It doesn't matter what he wears," Luke said, "it matters how Randy cooks."

"You'll meet Randy after we eat," Tom said.

"How come nobody else is here?" Clint asked.

"The place really ain't open yet, but there'll be some lumberjacks in here later," Tom explained. "What we gotta do is keep the cattlemen out."

"Their money would help keep the place going," Clint said. "Wouldn't it?"

"Yeah, it would," Tom said, "but then we'd have to let Harry Boyce in."

"Ah, Boyce," Clint said. "I've heard a little about him."

"He's the one who's makin' us have this contest," Tom said. "makin' us all compete for this job, instead of just picking the right people for it."

"And the right people would be?" Clint asked.

"Us!" Tom and Luke said, together.

***

Five men entered the saloon that Clint, Tom and Luke has just left. They all wore guns, and were obviously not lumber men.

As they approached the bar, the other men in the place turned and watched them.

"Five beers," one of them said. His name was Frank Titleman, and he was the leader of the group.

"What are you doin' here?" Blackie asked them. "Lookin' for trouble?"

"We're lookin' for cold beer, bartender," Titleman said. "Ain't that what you got, here?"

"The saloon down the street has it, too," Blackie said. "And that's the cattleman's saloon."

"Yeah, well we heard you had good beer over here, where the lumberjacks drink, and we wanted to check and see how good it is. Is that a problem?"

"As long as there's no trouble."

"Why would we cause trouble?" one of the other men asked. His name was Jensen, and he was a known troublemaker on the Boyce cow crew.

"So how about those beers?" Titleman asked.

"Comin' up," Blackie said.

Titleman turned and looked at the saloon that was half filled with lumber men. He picked up his beer, sipped it, and then spat it out onto the floor. The other men with him did the same.

"This tastes like piss," Titleman said.

"Now, wait a minute—" Blackie said, but he stopped when the man turned on him, his gun suddenly in his hand.

The lumberjacks in the saloon all stood up, some of their chairs falling over behind them.

"Hold it!" Jensen yelled, as he and the others pulled their guns and pointed them. "First man that moves gets it!"

"What's goin' on, Frank?" Blackie asked.

"You took the wrong side, Blackie," Titleman said. "We're just here to show you that."

"Oh yeah? How?"

Titleman smiled.

"All this fresh new wood? It'd go up with the first sign of a flame."

"You wouldn't do that," Blackie said.

"Why not?"

"Why would you?" the bartender asked. "Did your boss tell you to?"

"Mr. Boyce?" Titleman asked. "He don't even know we're here."

"Well then, he wouldn't like it," Blackie said. "He needs the lumberjacks."

"But he don't need this place," Titleman said.

"You burn this place down," Blackie said, "and none of your boss' trees will get cut down. None of the lumber men will work for him."

Titleman stared at Blackie, who seemed more pissed than scared.

"Ah!" he said, holstering his gun. "I'm just funnin' with ya, Blackie." He looked at the other men. "Put your guns up boys and let's get outta here."

They all holstered their guns and went out through the batwing doors, laughing and slapping each other on the backs.

SIX

The steaks were as thick as promised, cooked to perfection, smothered in onions, and accompanied by vegetables and biscuits.

"I think I want another one," Luke said.

Clint looked at the man's plate. It was empty, while his steak was only half gone.

"Jesus, Luke..." Tom said. "Yeah, okay." He waved the waiter over. "Danny, have Randy make another one for Big Luke, will ya?"

"With pleasure, Mr. Allen," Danny said.

Clint noticed that the man almost winced whenever Tom called him Danny.

"He doesn't like being called that, huh?"

"In Kansas City," Tom said, "they called him 'Daniel.'"

"You must be paying him a lot to get him to leave his job in Kansas City."

Luke was still working on the vegetables and onions that were left in his plate.

"He was gonna get fired, anyway."

"That so?" Clint asked.

Luke shrugged. "That's what he said."

"Well," Clint said, cutting into the half a steak that was left, "you better pay whatever you have to pay to keep this cook. This steak is the best."

"We know," Tom said. "We're keepin' him, believe me."

Clint and Tom finished their meals, then sat back and watched Luke eat his second steak, while they worked on fresh beers.

"Okay," Clint said, "tell me about the accidents."

"The branch," Luke said.

"We were out there on Boyce's and, takin' a look at the set-up, when a branch fell from a pine, almost hitting me."

"How big a branch?"

"As thick as you," Luke said. "And a branch like that don't usually fall without a crack."

"There was no noise?"

"None," Tom said.

"So, somebody dropped it?"

"You'd think so," Tom said, "but we looked up and couldn't see anyone."

"What about the thing with the buckboard?"

"That was a loose team..." Tom said, shaking his head.

"That wasn't a loose team," Luke said, with a mouthful of steak. "They tried to run him down."

"You saw somebody?" Clint asked.

"Didn't see anybody either time," Tom said.

"How long ago?"

"Within the last two weeks," Luke said.

"When was the last one?" Clint asked.

"The loose team was last week," Tom said.

"Nothing since?"

"No," Tom said.

Clint looked at Luke. "Who do you think is behind it?"

"Me? I think it's somebody workin' for Boyce."

"Why are you askin' him?" Tom asked.

"Because you seem to want to believe it's all accidental."

"Why would Boyce do it?" Tom asked. "He wants his trees cut down."

"There's lot of men who can do the job."

"Not the way I can."

"I didn't say Boyce," Luke inserted, "I said somebody workin' for him."

"So you don't think this was on his orders?"

"Maybe not," Luke said. "He's got men workin' for him that don't like lumber men. They put us in the same class as sheep herders."

"Not a good class to be in," Clint said. "I mean, from the point of view of cow men."

Luke put the last hunk of meat into his mouth and shoved his plate away. There was a fresh beer sitting there waiting for him. He grabbed it.

"So what's next?" he asked.

"We head back to the saloon," Tom said. "We've got to fill Clint in on what's gonna happen when the competition starts."

"Yeah," Clint said, "and I'd like to know everybody who doesn't want you to win."

"I told him," Luke said to Tom, "every other man who's competing."

"How many outfits want this contract?" Clint asked.

"There are five of us, and we're each sending two or three men in to compete."

"How many men do you have working for you, Tom?" Clint asked.

Tom and Luke exchanged a glance, and then Tom looked at Clint. "You're lookin' at them."

"Just the two of you?"

"Until we get the job," Tom said, "then I'll have the money to hire a crew."

"And the other outfits that you're competing against?"

"Oh, they have crews," Luke said.

"Tom, what made you think you'd get this job from Boyce?"

"Luke and I are a little more modern thinkin' when it comes to our methods, Clint. I think we can do a helluva job up here, and make a name for ourselves."

"So this job is very important to you?"

"Real important," Tom said. "It's my future."

"Well," Clint said, "I guess I'll have to do my best to keep you alive, and then you'll have to take it from there and do your best."

Tom picked up the remainder of his beer and held the mug up. Luke and Clint followed.

"Here's to doin' our best," he said.

As they stood up to leave, Clint asked, "Do you have men in mind for your crew?"

"Oh yeah," Tom said, "there's plenty up here lookin' for work, and plenty of others who would switch crews. And a lot of them are usually sittin' over in the saloon."

"Must be the fella who gave me a hard time when I got here," Clint said.

"Well, we'll change that," Tom said. "Let's go over there and have a drink, and show the rest of them that you're one of us."

They left the club and headed for the saloon.

SEVEN

As Clint, Tom and Luke approached the saloon they saw five men coming out, laughing and slapping one another on the back.

"Uh-oh," Luke said.

"That doesn't look good," Tom said.

"Who are they?" Clint asked.

"Looks like five of Harry Boyce's cowhands," Tom said.

"They look more like gunhands," Clint said.

"They wouldn't have to be real good with a gun to be a gunhand up here," Luke said. "Most of us are better with an axe than a gun."

"Well," Tom said, "at least we didn't hear any shootin'."

"But the only reason they'd come over here is to look for trouble," Tom commented. "All the cowhands drink over at the other saloon."

"They're all walkin'," Luke said. "If they did go hand-to-hand with the logger, they'd be limpin'."

"Let's go inside and find out," Tom said.

The three men mounted the boardwalk and entered through the batwings.

"Everybody okay in here?" Tom called out. "We just saw Boyce's men leavin'."

"We're okay," one of the men said, from the back.

"But if they'd stayed a little longer they wouldn'ta been. We woulda took them apart."

Blackie, the bartender, was in front of the bar with a mop.

"They just came in to make bad remarks about my beer," he said.

"They dumped good beer on the floor?" Luke asked.

"They spit it out," Blackie said.

"Jesus!" Luke said. "That's blasphemous!"

Blackie took his mop with him back behind the bar.

"Get you gents somethin'?"

"Three beers, Blackie," Tom said.

"And we won't be spittin' them out," Luke assured him.

Blackie quickly drew three mugs and set them up on the bar.

"They just came in to be nasty," Blackie said.

One of the lumber men came walking over to the bar.

"They pulled their irons," he said, "or they wouldn'ta walked out so healthy."

"Blackie, get Ed a beer."

"Comin' up."

"Thanks, Tom," Ed said.

"Ed, this is my friend, Clint Adams."

"Mr. Adams," Ed said. "I heard of ya. You here to become a lumberjack?"

"I'm just here to make sure Tom stays healthy enough to compete," Clint said.

Ed grabbed his fresh beer from the bar.

"Well, I'm one of them who thinks he can win the whole thing, and if he does I'll be the first to sign onto his crew. Thanks for the beer, Tom."

Ed walked back to his table.

"Ed's a good man," Tom said.,

"What's he do?" Clint asked.

"He's a gandy dancer," Luke said.

"What's a gandy dancer?"

"Usually a pick–and-axe man," Tom said. "They also work on railroads."

"Why are they called that?"

Both men laughed and Tom said, "Nobody knows."

"But that's what they are," Luke said.

Clint shrugged. Probably made as much sense as a lot of nicknames he'd heard for jobs.

"Who was the talker for that group?" Tom asked Blackie?

"Frankie Titleman," Blackie said. "He's got a big mouth."

"He's good with a gun, though," Tom said.

"Yeah," Luke said, "he's the one who could be called a gunman in that crew."

"Titleman?" Clint said. "I never heard of him."

"Spends most of his time up here," Tom said. "Boyce pays him well."

"Any chance these were the guys responsible for your accidents?" Clint asked.

"I don't see how they could've had anythin' to do with the tree branch," he said, "but the loose buckboard? Who knows?"

"Maybe," Clint said, "I should have a talk with this Titleman."

"I'll go with you," Luke said.

"Seems to me you'd just be lookin' for trouble," Tom said. "Maybe now that you're here, there won't be any more accidents, and we can just get on with the games."

"How many events are there?"

"There's chopping, sawing," Luke said, ticking them off on fingers like sausages, "axe throwing, log rolling and pole climbing."

"So five in all?"

"No," Tom said, "there are several different kinds of chopping and sawing. I'd say there's closer to a dozen events."

"In how many days?"

"Two."

"All that in two days?"

"It's about stamina, too," Tom said.

"And what if somebody gets hurt?" Clint said. "Cut, or... something."

"He's out," Luke said. "Unless he can compete with the injury."

"There's no time to recover?"

"None," Tom said.

"How many judges?"

"Three," Luke said, "and one of them is the head judge."

"He makes sure all the rules are followed, disqualifications are made fairly," Tom said.

"This is a lot more involved than I thought it would be," Clint said. "When does it start?"

"Day after tomorrow."

"So if somebody wants to knock you out of the competition," Clint said, "they've got the rest of today and all day tomorrow to get it done."

"But that ain't gonna happen," Tom, said, "because you're here."

"I'll drink to that!" Luke said.

EIGHT

It suddenly got very quiet in the saloon, which made Clint, Tom and Luke turn around to have a look.

The person standing just inside the doors was dressed like most of the men in the saloon: jeans, a plaid shirt, and boots. What was different was that it was a woman, not a man.

She was tall, almost six feet in her boots, with blonde hair and a full, solid, but still womanly body that had all the men staring.

She looked around, spotted somebody at the bar—Clint knew it wasn't him—then smiled and walked over.

"Hey, Tom."

"Hello, Sally."

She gave Tom a big hug, then looked at Luke. "Big, Luke! C'mere, you big lug."

Luke gave her a bear hug, lifting her off the ground, but it looked as if she gave as good as she got.

"Sally, this is my friend, Clint Adams," Tom said. "Clint, Sally Hayfield, as good a lumberjack as you'll find, man or woman."

She turned to face Clint, looked him up and down and smiled.

"Pleased to meet you, Mr. Adams."

"My pleasure, Sally."

They shook hands and he wasn't surprised at how

firm her grip was.

"Buy you a beer?" Clint asked.

"Why not?"

"I was wonderin' when you'd get here," Tom asked.

As Blackie slid her a beer, she grinned and said, "You didn't think I was just gonna hand you this job, did you?"

"Oh no," Tom said, "I knew I was gonna have to fight for it."

"Wait," Clint said, "you mean Sally's going to compete?"

"And why not?" Sally asked, looking at him. "You got a problem with a woman competing in a man's world?"

"Not at all," Clint said. "I thought, since you were friends, that you were part of the same crew."

"No," Sally said, "I've got my own business to worry about. But that doesn't mean that Tom, here," she said, slapping Tom on the shoulder, "and me can't still be friends."

"Friends?" Clint asked, looking at Tom.

"Just friends," Tom said. "Blackie, another round."

***

They gravitated to a table, and the four of them sat and drank while others came and went in and out of the saloon.

"So what's your best event?" Clint asked. "Not that I know what all the events even involve."

"We can show you tomorrow," Luke said. "We'll take you out to where it's all gonna happen."

"And me?" Sally said. "I'm good at all of it. Every event."

"How can you do that?" Clint asked.

"You'll see," she said. "Me, Tom, Luke, we'll be in all of 'em."

"Yeah," Luke said, "all we gotta do is drink enough."

"If you guys try this drunk," Tom said, drunk himself, "you'll end up losing an arm or a leg."

"Maybe just a finger," Luke said. He held up his left hand, and for the first time Clint noticed it was missing a little finger. "That wouldn't be so bad, right?"

"Ask Clint," Tom said. "If he lost his trigger finger he wouldn't be the Gunsmith, anymore."

"The Gunsmith!" Sally said, her eyes widened. She pointed at Clint. "That's who you are. I knew I heard your name before." She reached out and clamped her hand on his shoulder. "Lemme buy you a drink."

"I've had enough," Clint said. "In fact, I think we all had enough."

"He's right," Tom said. "Time to get some sleep. Luke, you got a room?"

"I slept in the barn last night."

"You can sleep on the floor in mine, then," Tom said. "Sally?"

"Don't worry about me," she said. "I always got someplace to sleep."

"Then let's get out of here."

They left the saloon, Tom and Luke leaning on each other, Sally hanging onto Clint's left arm, and Tom's right. Linked that way, they staggered to the hotel.

***

When they reached the hotel, Clint offered to walk Sally to wherever she was staying.

"Don't worry about me," she said. "Just get these two baboons to their room safe. I'll see you all tomorrow."

So Clint staggered into the hotel lobby with Tom and Luke, leaving Sally standing outside.

"Oh, uh, Mr. Adams," the clerk said, "we don't have another room for your friend—"

"Don't worry about it, Terry," Tom said. "He's sleepin' on the floor in mine."

"Oh," Terry said, "okay, then. Uh, good-night."

Clint helped them get up the stairs and down the hall to room 11. Once inside he and Tom got Luke to the bed and dropped him onto it. He immediately started to snore.

"Ah crap," Tom said, "looks like maybe I'm the one sleepin' on the floor."

"You want me to help you get him off the bed?" Clint asked.

"Nah, nah," Tom said, "leave 'im. You go to your room and I'll see you in the mornin' for breakfast—that little café where you had a sandwich. Okay?"

"You got it," Clint said. "See you then."

Clint turned to leave and Tom clamped his hand onto his left arm.

"I'm really glad you came, Clint."

"Me, too, Tom. Good-night."

He went down the hall to room 7 and let himself in.

***

He hadn't had as much to drink as Tom and Luke, so he didn't fall asleep right away. He had time to get his boots off, rub his feet a bit. After that he spent some time cleaning his guns. If he was going to need them, he had to make sure they were in proper working order.

After that he walked to the window and looked out. All he could see was a dark alley. It occurred to him that while riding in, he had not seen a bank building, nor a sheriff's office. Was there no law in this nameless town? Or was there just no law, yet?

When the knock came at his door he shook his head and grabbed his gun. It seemed like the only time he ever got to rest without somebody knocking on his door—whether it was good news or bad—was when he was camped out.

He went to the door, gun in hand, and asked, "Who is it?"

"Sally."

He was surprised. When he'd left her outside she'd supposedly been heading to bed for the night.

He opened the door a crack, saw her standing there alone, and opened it the rest of the way.

"Is there a problem?" he asked. "I thought you were headed to bed."

"I don't have a room," she said.

"But you said you had a place to sleep."

"I do," she said, with a smile. "Here."

NINE

"Wha—"

"Can I come in?"

"Um, well—"

"You got a girl in there, already?"

"No, but—"

"Then you're alone."

"Yes."

"Then can I come in?" she asked, again.

"Okay."

He stepped aside to allow her to enter, then took a quick look in the hall to be sure it was empty.

"I didn't bring anybody," she said, as he closed the door. "You won't need that." She indicated his gun.

"You can never be too careful." He walked to the bedpost and put it back into the holster hanging there. "What's this about, Sally?"

"It's about you, and me, sleepin' together," she said. "Unless the idea doesn't appeal to you."

"No, of course not--I mean, it does, but—"

"And just to be clear, I don't mean just sleepin'."

"Sally—"

"Don't I appeal to you?" she asked. "Don't tell me you're afraid of strong women."

"I love strong women, but—"

"Good," she said, "then you're gonna love me. Have

a seat on the bed."

Helpless, he sat. Reasoning that he did love strong women, and she did appeal to him. And she appeared to be very willing, if not eager. So why turn her away?

"Watch," she said, and started to unbutton her shirt. "I've spent a lot of years on this body, makin' sure it wouldn't betray me at the wrong time. So I made sure there wasn't a weak point, anywhere."

She whipped off the shirt and tossed it away. Now naked to the waist she put her hands on her hips, posing. She had impressive breasts, large and hard looking, powerful arms, not an inch of fat anywhere on her pale torso.

"I have to have good upper body strength for chopping, and sawing, and climbing," she said, undoing her pants, "but also a powerful lower body. That means my thighs and my legs." She slid her trousers down to her ankles. He noticed she wore no undergarments, at all. She was right about her thighs and legs, they were exceptionally strong looking, and beautiful.

"I haven't had a bath in a few days," she said, "I might smell a bit. I hope you don't mind."

"You smell fine to me," he said. She smelled like the outdoors, and like a woman who was ready for a man. In fact, the blonde hair at her crotch seemed darker than the hair on her head, made so because it was already slightly damp.

"Would you help me with my boots?" she asked.

"Of course."

She sat at the foot of the bed and he rose, walked to her and crouched in front of her, where her scent came to him even stronger.

She held her legs up so he could slide off her boots, and then he took her trousers from around her ankles and tossed them away. He looked up at her face, framed by the blonde hair that fell around it to her shoulders.

"You're beautiful," he said.

She smiled. "Probably not, but I'm the way I need to be to do my job. But I also feel I'm the way I want to be to satisfy a man, and myself."

"Well, I'm satisfied,"

"Not yet," she said, "but you will be. Stand up."

He obeyed, and she undid his belt and slid down his trousers and underwear until they were around his ankles.

"Oh, my," she said, as his hard cock stood at attention.

"You'll be satisfied, too," he told her.

She giggled and said, "I think so."

She took his cock in both of her hands, stroked it for a few moments, then slid one down to cup his balls.

"You're very pretty," she said. "I've seen a lot of men with big, ugly, veiny things between their legs, but this... you're so smooth, and pretty."

"Thank you."

She began to stroke him with more vigor, actually closing one hand around him and pumping him.

"I'd like to play with this some more another time," she said, "but right now I'd like us to get into bed together. Is that okay?"

"That's fine with me."

She stood up, and he saw that without her boots her height was still somewhat imposing, though nowhere near his six feet.

She turned, showing him her glorious ass, as she took his hand and led him over to the side of the bed. Pulling down the sheet, she slid in first, and he joined her. Intense body heat trapped his hardness between them as they kissed for the first time.

"Mmmm," she moaned, as their tongues entwined.

He broke the kiss, moved his lips to her neck and shoulders.

"You know," she said, "this isn't just so I'd have a place to sleep tonight."

"I know."

"That would make me a whore."

"I never thought that," he said, moving down to kiss her breasts.

She cupped his head in her hands as he tongued her nipples, then bit and sucked them.

"Oh, yeah," she said, "when I walked into the saloon and saw you with those two baboons, I knew..."

"Knew what?"

"That we'd end up here," she said, "and that it would be good. I could tell."

"Well," he said, "I'll try not to disappoint you."

As he moved down her body until his face was nestled in her blonde pubic patch she said, "Oh, I know you won't..."

TEN

When Clint nestled in with his face pressed to Sally's crotch he tongued her until she was soaking wet, then worked on her with his fingers, lips and tongue at the same time. Before long she arched her back, lifted her butt up off the bed and bit back a scream of pleasure as wave after wave washed over her.

"Oh God," she said, when she was able to speak. "That was even better than I expected."

"Glad to hear it."

"Come up here, you!"

He moved up next to her and she grabbed him and kissed him, tasting herself on his mouth and face.

"Now lie still," she said, climbing astride him. "Let Sally do the work."

She sat on him, her hot crotch pressing his cock down against his belly. Slowly, she began to rub herself up and down on it as she leaned down to kiss him again, pushing her tongue into his mouth, moaning.

He put his arms around her, ran his hands down her powerful back.

After her pussy had wet the length of him, she lifted her hips just long enough to reach down and guide him into her.

"Oh, damn," she said, as she sat down on him, taking him fully inside.

39

"Jesus—" he gasped, as the heat of her closed around him.

She began to move up and down on him, her hands pressed down against his chest. He put his hands on her hips as she sat up and began to literally jump up and down on him.

She began to gasp and moan, and at one point she actually put one hand over her mouth to muffle her own cries.

Clint felt his own shout building in his throat, turning his head to try and muffle it with the pillow. When that didn't work he found himself painfully biting his lip.

At one point the bed began to bounce up and down on the floor, and Clint hoped it wouldn't bring the clerk up to see what was happening.

She put her hands down on him again, on his belly this time, but not flat. Her hands were claws, and her nails dug into his flesh. He barely felt it, though, because his orgasm was rushing up from his legs into his crotch, and then he was gushing inside of her as she continued to move on him, milking him until his ejaculations were almost painful...

...and then they were, and it didn't matter...

***

"Satisfied?" she asked, moments later. She was lying next to him, trying to catch her breath.

"Very," he said. "Ready to go to sleep?"

"I am," she said, reaching down and digging her fingers into his thigh, "for now..."

ELEVEN

lint woke with Sally's thigh over his. He was content to lie there that way for a while, her body's heat keeping him warm, but at that moment somebody started pounding on his door.

"Clint!" a man shouted. "Come on, you gotta get up! Somethin's happened!"

"What's that?" Sally muttered.

"Somebody at the door," Clint said, moving her leg off of him.

He quit the bed, padded to the door barefoot with his gun in his hand.

"Clint, it's me, Luke. Tom sent me to get you."

Clint opened the door, and the big man filled the door frame.

"What's going on?" he asked.

"There's been a murder."

"What?"

"A killin'."

"Who?"

"Ed." Luke saw the blank look on Clint's face. "The gandy dancer."

"Oh," Clint said, "what happened, a saloon brawl?"

"No," Luke said, "somebody just killed him. Come on, Tom's waitin'."

"Is there any law in this town?" Clint asked.

"No," Luke said, "just us."

"Okay," Clint said, "let me get my pants on."

He closed the door. If Luke had managed to spy Sally in his bed behind him, the big man hadn't said a word.

"What's goin' on?" Sally demanded.

"Somebody got killed," he said. "Tom wants me."

"Tom and Luke are okay?" she asked, sitting up. The sheet fell away, revealing her pale, large breasts. Even soft, her pink nipples were very large.

"Yes, they're fine," he said, pulling on his pants.

"I better get dress—" she started to say, swinging her legs off the bed.

"Why don't you stay here?" he suggested. "There's nothing you can do, and we'll let you know what happens."

"Okay." She got back into bed, covered up with the sheet. "Be careful."

"I'll see you later."

As he went to the door, strapping on his gun, she asked, "Is it somebody I know?"

"A fella named Ed?"

"Not the gandy dancer?"

"That's him."

"Shit," she said, swinging her legs off the bed again. "I'm comin'."

***

Luke led Clint and Sally to an alley that ran along one side of the saloon. There they found Tom Allen standing next to the body of Ed, the gandy dancer.

"Somebody cut him up real bad," Tom said. "Looks like the work of an axe."

Clint took a look. He'd never seen a man who had

been cut that way, and he never wanted to see another one. While Ed's face had been spared, his body bore many deep cuts, any one of which could have probably killed him.

"Is there a lawman in town?" Clint asked, knowing what the answer was going to be.

"No," Tom said.

"Like I told you," Luke said, "it's just us."

"You and Tom keep the law?" Clint asked.

"He means all of us," Sally said. "We handle things ourselves."

"Things like murder?" Clint asked.

"Well... we ain't never had a murder, until now," Sally admitted.

Clint looked down at Ed, whose blood had soaked into the dirt around him.

"Who found him?" he asked.

"I did," Tom said.

"How did you happen to look in this alley?"

"Just glanced in here as I passed," Tom said. "I don't know, maybe I felt somethin'."

"Is there an undertaker in town, at least?" Clint asked.

"Yeah," Luke said. "He gets plenty of work from accidents, from both the lumber men and the cowhands."

"All right," Clint said, "we'll have to get Ed—does he have a last name?"

"Fenner," Tom said.

"We'll have to get Mr. Fenner covered, and then moved to the undertaker's."

"I can get some men—" Tom said.

"No," Clint said. "If we're going to have to handle this ourselves, then let's keep the people who know about it to a minimum. Just those of us here. Let's get him covered and then try to carry him to the undertaker's without being seen."

"It still might be early enough for that," Tom said.

"If we move fast," Clint said.

"I know where there's a tarp," Luke said. "I'll be right back."

Luke ran off, leaving Clint, Tom and Sally to stand around Ed Fenner's body.

"He would have joined your crew if you got the job?" Clint asked Tom.

Tom looked at Sally, then said, "I think so."

"Whoever got the job," Sally said, "would have hired Ed. "He was a good worker."

"So killing him wouldn't hurt either of your chances, right?" Clint asked.

"I don't see how," Tom said.

"No, not mine," Sally said.

"Was he going to compete?"

"Not Ed," Tom said. "He was just gonna wait to see who won."

"Can we count on the undertaker to keep this quiet?"

"If he wants to stay in business," Tom said.

They waited the rest of the time in an awkward silence until Luke returned with a tarp.

***

They hurriedly carried the wrapped body to the undertaker's office before anybody else had hit the streets. With Luke and Tom holding the body, Sally banged on the front door until the man opened it.

"What the—"

"We got some work for you, Millard," Tom said.

"This early? Well, come on in, then."

The undertaker was in his fifties, a very pale man

with only wisps of hair left on his head.

"Clint, this is Millard Winston. Millard, this is Clint Adams."

"The Gunsmith?" the undertaker said. "I heard you was in town. Kill somebody, already, didja?"

"No," Clint said, shortly.

"Clint didn't do this," Tom said. "We don't know who did."

"Well, bring him in the back."

Clint let Tom and Luke carry the body into the back and explain the situation to the undertaker.

"Jesus," Sally said, "who'd want to kill poor Ed like that?"

"Unless we can get a lawman up here," Clint said, "I guess that's what we're going to have to find out."

TWELVE

Tom and Luke got the situation explained to Millard Winston, who agreed to keep it to himself.

"I don't need to know who killed him in order to do my job," he said.

The two men washed their hands to get Ed's blood off them, and then the four of them left the undertaker's office, stopping just outside on the boardwalk. Now there were a few people making their way to start their days.

"Anybody hungry after seeing that?" Sally asked.

"I'm starved," Luke said.

"Me, too," Tom said.

"I could eat," Clint commented.

"Oh good," she said. "I thought it was just me."

They made their way over to the small café where Clint had eaten his sandwich. They were the first customers of the day, and took a table in the back. When the waiter came out they all ordered eggs with their own preference of breakfast meats. And coffee.

Once they had coffee Clint asked, "What's the nearest town with law?"

"That'd be Cascade," Tom said.

"How far?"

"A hundred miles, maybe more."

"Nothing closer?"

"There's still a lot of this area that ain't been settled," Sally said.

"So," Clint said, "four days to get a lawman here."

"By then the competition will almost be over," Tom said. "Nobody's gonna want to ride to Cascade and miss it."

"I could," Clint said. "On my horse, Eclipse, I could do it faster."

"Maybe you'd get there sooner," Tom said, "but a lawman on another horse other than yours?" He shook his head. "Still take him two days to get back here."

"So what do you suggest?" Clint asked.

"Well, you came here to support me," Tom said. "Now you've decided you have to protect me, keep me alive. Part of that might be finding out who killed Ed."

Clint was about to say he wasn't a detective, but according to his friend Talbot Roper, who was a private detective, he had all the qualities. He had solved some murders before, so why not this one?

"You'll have to help me," he said. "All of you."

"Well," Tom said, "you've got us for the rest of the day. But tomorrow everythin' starts."

"If we're gonna play detective," Luke said, "why don't we start with the saloon?"

"Is it open?" Clint asked.

"That's the thing about this place," Sally said. "The saloons are always open."

"Then after we eat," Clint said, "let's go."

***

Once in the saloon, which was empty except for Blackie, when they were set up with beers, they told the bartender what had happened.

48

"Ed's dead?" he said. "Jesus, he was here last night."

"Everybody was here last night, Blackie," Tom said.

"What time did he leave?" Clint asked.

"I think he was the last one to leave," Blackie said. "Maybe around two?"

Clint looked at Sally.

"I thought you said the saloon is always open."

"It is," Blackie said, "but nobody came in after two, until the four of you."

"Did Ed have an argument with anybody last night?" Clint asked.

"Not last night," Blackie said, "but he and some of the other boys, they're always arguin', you know. In a good natured away. Or they argue with the cowhands in a not so good natured way."

"I'll need the names of these men," Clint said.

"I don't know the cow hands' names," Blackie said, "except for the ones you saw yesterday. Titleman, Jensen and them."

"Then I'll start with them," Clint said, "and Ed's friends."

"You think he was killed by a friend?" Sally asked.

"He was killed by somebody who knew him."

"What makes you say that?" Luke asked.

"The way he was hacked up," Clint said. "Somebody was mad as hell at him."

"Geez," Blackie said, "I think I need a drink." He grabbed a bottle and a shot glass.

"Make that five," Tom said.

"And Blackie," Clint said, as the man poured five drinks, "keep this quiet. I don't want the killer to know we're after him. Let him think he got away with it in a town with no law."

"Okay," Blackie said.

49

They all downed their shots.

***

After leaving the saloon Clint said, "Let's go over to the other saloon."

"This early?" Tom asked. "There won't be any cowhands there."

"Let's check anyway," Clint said. "Talk to the bartender."

"That'd be Jake," Luke said.

"What's he like?" Clint asked.

"He's a hard head," Luke said, "likes cow men, hates lumber men."

"But," Tom said, with a big grin, "he likes Sally."

Clint looked at Sally.

"What's not to like?" she asked, with a smile.

"Okay, then," Clint said. "Let's talk to Jake the bartender. If he wants to play it hard, we'll send in Sally."

"The big gun!" Luke said, with a grin.

"The biggest," she said.

They started across the street to the other saloon without a name.

THIRTEEN

The second saloon in town was also newly built and spanking clean. Inside, however, it was clear that the clientele was different. There were many steer heads and horns hanging on the walls, and horns also hanging from the ceiling on several chandeliers. Obviously, more money had gone into this place than the lumber men's saloon, and that was because the money had come from the ranchers.

"Lotta cow money in here," Tom said, as they entered. "In fact, most of it is Harry Boyce's. He wanted his men to have a place to relax."

At the moment, however, there were no ranch hands in the place. It was much too early, and cowhands were at work. The only people in the saloon were a bartender, and two bored looking saloon girls.

Clint, Tom, Luke and Sally walked to the bar. The bartender, Jake, looked up from what he was doing and seemed surprised.

"What the hell are you guys doin' here?" he asked.

"We got a new friend in town," Tom said. "He wanted to come and see what you got here."

"Jake," Luke said, "meet Clint Adams."

Jake was looking at Sally, but when he heard Clint's name he looked at him.

"Adams? The Gunsmith?"

"That's right," Tom said. "He came up to see the lumberjack competition."

"And I'm anxious to taste your beer," Clint said.

"Oh, uh, beer," Jake said, "coming up."

"Make it four beers," Clint said. "I want to drink with my friends."

"Sure thing, Mr. Adams."

Jake set four beer up on the bar. The two saloon girls at the other end of the bar sensed that something was happening. One was brunette, one had red hair, and they both straightened up and paid attention.

Clint tasted the beer, found it as cold and as good as it had been at the first saloon.

"Pretty good," Clint said.

"Thanks," Jake said.

"I'm looking for another friend of mine," Clint said, "an these folks can't help me find him."

"Who would that be?" Jake asked. He was in his fifties, barrel-chested, with scarred hands that betrayed the fact that he had not always tended bar.

"His name's Ed," Clint said, "Ed Fenner?"

"Fenner?" Jake shook his head. "I don't know him. What's he do? Is he a cowhand?"

"No," Clint said, "He works lumber. He's a gandy dancer."

"Oh," Jake said, "well, these folks'll tell you, this saloon's for cowhands."

"I just thought maybe you might have seen him last night," Clint said.

Jake shook his head. "Wouldn't even know what he looks like. Gandy dancer? What is that?"

"It doesn't matter," Clint said. He looked down the bar at the two girls. "Either of you know who Ed Fenner is?"

The two girls shook their head, and the brunette said, "No, sir, but if you want, we can go upstairs and talk about it."

Sally put her arm though Clint's and said, "He don't have time for that, girlie."

Clint drank half his beer and set the mug down on the bar. Tom and Luke had finished theirs. Sally's was hardly touched.

"Thanks for the beer," Clint said. "On the house, right?"

"Definitely," Jake said, "on the house for the Gunsmith and his friends."

"Good-bye, ladies," Clint said to the saloon girls.

"Don't be a stranger," the brunette called to the four of them, as they went out the front door.

"Bitch," Sally said.

"Be nice, Sally," Luke said.

"I just thought of somethin'," Tom said.

"What's that?" Clint asked.

"Isn't it gonna be hard to investigate Ed's murder without tellin' people he's dead?"

"Good point," Clint said. "Eventually, it'll get around, but let's do it one person at a time."

"So who's the next person?" Sally asked.

"That depends," Clint said. "Where would everybody be, right now?"

"They're probably still getting the events together," Tom said. "Some down by the river, others in the area we chose for the chopping, sawing and climbing events."

"Can we go there?" Clint asked.

"Definitely," Tom said. "That was on my schedule, anyway, to take you down there so you could have a look."

"What about the judges?" Clint asked. "Have they

already been chosen?"

"They have."

"And where are they?"

"Well," Tom said, "two of them live near here, and one of them is stayin' in the same hotel that we are."

"Our hotel clerk said the place is filled," Clint said. "Where else are people staying?"

"They're doubling and tripling up in the hotel, some are camping out, other are using a barn, or the livery, or are paying somebody to use a room in their homes."

"Are there many homes near here?"

"They're popping up all the time," Tom said. "A lot of us are taking jobs building them while we're waitin' to see who gets the Boyce job."

"That's interesting," Clint said. "Do you all have horses?"

"I do," Tom said.

"I have a buckboard," Sally said.

"I'll ride with Sally," Luke said.

"Okay," Clint said, "let's get saddled up and meet in front of the livery."

FOURTEEN

Tom Allen led the way to a clearing about five miles outside of town—it was a natural clearing that had been cultivated, and widened, and set up to host the competition of lumberjacks. While many trees had been cleared away, others had obviously been left for the climbing part of the contest. Other areas had been set up for the chopping and sawing contests.

They dismounted and walked across the field. There was still hammering and sawing going on, so Clint knew the field wasn't ready for use, yet.

"Will this be ready by tomorrow?" he asked.

"Should be," Tom said.

A couple of men began to laugh, looked over and waved at Sally. She waved back.

"Do any of you know who Ed's friends were?" Clint asked.

"I know a couple," Sally said.

"So do I," Luke added.

"See if they're here," Clint told them. "If they are, see what they know about what Ed was doing last night, who he was seen with."

"Can we tell them he's dead?" Luke asked.

"Only if you have to," Clint said, "but tell them not to spread the news around."

"Okay," Luke said.

"We'll meet back here in an hour," Clint added.

"Right," Sally said. She slapped Luke on the shoulder. "Let's go, big man."

"And what do we do?" Tom asked.

"Show me what they're doing down by the river," Clint said.

"Follow me."

***

When they came within sight of the river, it was below them. Clint saw that it was loaded with floating logs.

"That's the Rogue River," Tom said. "We'll be usin' that for the log rollin'."

"And you can do that?" Clint asked. "Walk on those logs?"

"Well, sure," Tom said. "Most lumber men can. And Sally."

"How hard is it?"

"That depends on the current," Tom said.

"So Ed wasn't going to do that."

"No," Tom said, "Ed was pick-and-axe. He did scut work. In fact, he would've been here working on setting up the events if he was still alive."

"How far is Harry Boyce's ranch from here?"

Tom pointed. "Over that ridge you'll already be on his land, and then it's about ten or twelve miles to the East."

"This side of the river."

"Oh, yeah."

"I've got an idea," Clint said. "You stay here, and if I'm not back in time, meet up with Luke and Sally like we said, in an hour."

"You goin' to Boyce's place?"

"Yes," Clint said, "just for a talk."

"You might have some trouble with his men," Tom said. "I could come and back you up."

"You any better with a gun than you used to be?"

"No," Tom admitted, "but I'm great with an axe."

"An axe against a gun just won't do it," Clint told him. "I'll be fine. Like I said, I just want to talk to him."

"If you run into Titleman—"

"I'll talk to him, too," Clint said, cutting him off. "Is he the ramrod?"

"No," Tom said, "Boyce's foreman is named Trapp, Lenny Trapp. Been workin' there a lot of years."

"How old is Boyce?"

"He's in his fifties," Tom said. "Trapp's about the same age."

"Wife, kids?"

"Both," Tom said, "he's got a wife, and a daughter."

"How heavily is he invested in getting this town up and running?" Clint asked.

"Without it he'd have to keep sending to Cascade for his supplies," Tom said. "Getting this town set up would help his business a lot."

"And he wants it named after him."

"That's right," Tom said. "Boyceville, or just Boyce."

"Is there a Mayor, yet?"

"No. A lot of the buildings have just been completed. They're empty. There's about half a dozen businesses in town—the hotel, two saloons, the undertaker, the livery, a leather shop—maybe as many as two or three more, but that's it."

"Even advertising," Clint said, "it'll take months to fill the town with citizens."

"And we'll be here, cutting his lumber," Tom said, "getting it ready to ship East for him."

"A murder's not good for anybody," Clint said.

"You gonna tell him about it?"

"I think I will," Clint said. "Would he have a motive to kill Ed?"

"None that I can think of," Tom said. "He only knows me, Sally, and some of the other guys with their own outfits. He doesn't know the workers."

"What about the other outfits?"

"I told you," Tom said, "whoever gets this job would've hired Ed. He's—he was a damned good worker."

"Okay," Clint said, "it doesn't sound like I'll have a whole lot of trouble. I should be back in time to meet up with you and the others, and then we can go back to town."

"Okay, well, we'll be here," Tom said, "and maybe we'll have some news."

They turned and headed back to where the horses were.

FIFTEEN

Clint followed Tom's directions and, before long, he came within sight of the house, barn and corral. From where he sat he could see it was a busy, working ranch. There were horses in the corral, and beyond the house he could see a herd of cattle. He decided to ride right down to the house.

As he approached, men turned to watch him. He'd been through this before and knew what was going on in their minds. Working on a ranch, you became part of a family—if you stayed long enough. When a stranger rode in, everybody took notice and wondered what was going to happen.

In front of the house he stopped, but didn't dismount. He knew that several men were walking over to him from the corral. He decided to wait.

"Can we help ya?" one man asked, as two others came into view. The speaker was a big man in his fifties, with an air of authority. Clint decided this was the foreman, Trapp.

"I'm here to see Mr. Boyce."

"You got business with him?" the man asked.

"I might."

"Well," the man said, "you gotta get past me before you see him. Convince me."

"Are you Trapp?"

"That's right. I'm the foreman."

"Well, my name's Clint Adams, and I'd like to see your boss."

Trapp digested that for a moment, with nothing showing on his face. The two men with him looked surprised. None of the three were armed.

"What's this about?"

"Tell him it has to do with the new town."

"What's that to you?" Trapp asked.

"I'll tell him."

Trapp didn't move.

"If he doesn't agree to see me," Clint said, "I won't even dismount."

"Wait here," Trapp said, after a moment. He started to walk away from the house.

"He's not in the house?" Clint called.

"Mr. Boyce is in the barn," one of the other men said, and the one beside him nudged him to keep quiet.

Clint watched Trapp walk to the barn and enter, and then come back out after two minutes. He walked back to where Clint was still mounted.

"Go back to work," he told the other two. To Clint he said, "Follow me."

He started to walk back to the barn, and Clint walked Eclipse behind him.

"The boss is inside," Trapp said. "I can take your horse—"

"Okay if I take him inside with me?"

"Yeah, sure."

Clint dismounted.

"Anybody else in there with Mr. Boyce?"

"Ben Foster."

"Who's he?"

"Nearest thing we got to a vet."

"Okay, thanks."

Clint walked in, leading Eclipse behind him.

"Tie your horse off right there, Mr. Adams, and come on over," a man said.

Clint assumed this was Harry Boyce. He was surprised. The man was in his fifties, and dressed like all the other hands on the ranch. Usually, the boss stood out from the employees, but if these men rode into town, you wouldn't be able to tell Boyce from his men.

Instead of tying Eclipse off, Clint simply grounded his reins, and then approached Boyce. The rancher was standing just outside a stall, watching another man work on a prone filly.

"She's in breach," he told Clint. "My man is tryin' to save her and the foal."

"And failing that?" Clint asked.

Boyce looked at Clint with one raised eyebrow. "The foal. What can I do for you, Mr. Adams? What's the Gunsmith doin' up in these

parts?"

"I have a friend who's competing for the contract to cut your lumber," Clint said.

"That so? Who would that be?"

"Tom Allen."

"Allen?" Boyce nodded. "He's a good man."

"Yes, he is. But if you think that, why have this competition for your contract?"

"Because I never give anything away, Mr. Adams," Boyce said. "That's not the way I do business. I believe men have to work—or fight—for what they get."

"I see."

The filly whinnied, attracting Boyce's attention.

"How's she doing, Foster?"

"I've got the foal turned, sir," Foster said. "She

should be giving birth any time now."

"Okay," Boyce said, "let me know when she does. I'll be at the house." He turned to Adams. "Will you come with me and have a drink?"

"Why not?"

"You can leave your horse here."

"I think I'll leave him in front of the house."

"Suit yourself."

They walked to the house, once again attracting the attention of some of the hands--and the foreman. Trapp was standing by the corral.

"I met your foreman," Clint said.

"That's as it should be," Boyce said. "He's my first line of defense. Come on, I've got some good bourbon inside."

SIXTEEN

lint expected Boyce to take him to an office, but instead he took him to a front room that was set up as a living room, with a sofa and two chairs set up around a large wooden coffee table, all in front of a stone fireplace. Then, in front of the window that looked out onto the corral and barn, there was a large oak desk. To the left of the desk was a small side bar, which Boyce approached.

"This is good stuff," he said, pouring two glasses. "I had it brought in from St. Louis." He handed Clint a glass. "Ever been to St. Louis?"

"I have, yes."

"Sure, you have," Boyce said, sipping his bourbon. "You travel around a lot, that's why you're known all over the West. Me, I never get away from here, except for a business trip or two."

"Maybe you should," Clint said.

"Oh yeah," Boyce said, "and then watch my business go to hell. Now, if I had a son to run things..." Boyce stopped, seemed to drift away for a moment, then came back to the present. "But I don't. I have a daughter, and she's not interested in my business."

"That's too bad."

"You don't know the half of it," Boyce said. "She left as soon as the town was built, started working in one of the saloons."

Clint immediately thought about the two saloon girls he'd seen in the cowhand's saloon. He wondered...

"Anyway," Boyce said, "you're not here for that. But for the life of me, I can't figure out why you are here, Mr. Adams. You can't be looking for a job."

"I'm not," Clint said. "I only came to watch the festivities and support Tom Allen, but..."

"But what?"

"... something's come up, and I'm being pressed into service because there's no lawman in town."

Boyce frowned. "What's happened?"

"There's been a murder."

"That's... awful. Who was killed?"

"One of the lumber men," Clint said. "I'm not giving out his name just yet, but... I'm wondering how your men get along with the lumber boys."

"They don't like them," Boyce said, "but then they don't like each other, do they?"

"What about a fella named Titleman?"

"Frank? You think Frank did it?"

"I didn't say that," Clint said, "I just asked... what about him. Is he a troublemaker?"

"He's a good worker," Boyce said, "when he's here. That's all I care about. If he gets into trouble when he's on his own time, well, that's his own business."

"I see," Clint said. "I'm told he's good with a gun. Is that why you hired him?"

"Not exactly," Boyce said. "Not strictly speaking, but it's always good to have somebody around who can use one." Boyce frowned. "Was the dead man shot?"

"No," Clint said, "he was killed with an axe."

"Well then, that would point to a lumberjack, wouldn't it?" Boyce asked.

"Maybe it would," Clint said, "or maybe it's just supposed to."

"I have to tell you," Boyce said, "I don't see why any of my men would kill a lumberjack. There's no profit in it, that I can see. Is that what you came here to ask me?"

"I'm just starting to ask questions, Mr. Boyce," Clint said, "thought I'd include you in the process."

"I don't recall detective being part of the legend of the Gunsmith, Mr. Adams."

"Like I said," Clint replied, "I'm being pressed into service."

The front door opened and moments after Ben Foster appeared. He was covered with blood and other fluids.

"She give birth, Mr. Boyce," he said.

"What is it?"

"A colt, like you wanted."

"Yes!" Boyce said. He put his glass down. "I've got to go and have a look, Mr. Adams. You want to come along?"

"I don't think so," Clint said, setting his own glass down. "I think I've taken up enough of your time."

"I wish you luck with your endeavor, then," Boyce said.

They walked out together. On the porch Clint asked, "You mind if I talk to your foreman, maybe some of your men?"

"You go on ahead," Boyce said, "but I won't order them to talk to you. That'll be up to them."

"That's fine."

"Good day to you, then."

Boyce hurried along, following his almost-a-vet to the barn.

Clint didn't have to look for the foreman. Trapp came walking over to him.

"You done?" he asked.

"I might have a few more questions," Clint said.

"My men are busy."

"For you, then," Clint said.

"I doubt Mr. Boyce would order me to talk to you."

"No, he said it'd be up to you."

"I got nothin' to say, then."

"You don't know the subject."

Trapp smirked.

"Word gets around."

"So you know about the killing?"

"Like I said, word gets around. You ain't gonna find your killer out here, but I can't say it pains me to have a lumberjack turn up dead."

"It should bother you to have any man turn up dead," Clint said.

"A man with your reputation has the nerve to say that to me?" Trapp demanded.

"You're old enough to know what a reputation is worth, Trapp," Clint said.

"So ask your questions, then."

"Do you know Ed Fenner?"

"Never heard of him."

"Think any of your men know him?"

"I doubt it."

"Why?"

"Because we drink in different saloons," Trapp said.

"Except that I saw five of your men in the lumberjack saloon just yesterday."

Trapp didn't like that. "What? Who?"

"Titleman," Clint said, "A fella name Jensen, and a few others. Seems to me they were looking for trouble."

"My men have orders to stay away from that place," Trapp said. "Those boys are gonna hear about this from me, but that still don't mean they killed some lumberjack with an axe. In fact, if Titleman killed him, he'd use a gun."

"That's what I hear," Clint said, "that Titleman fancies himself a hand with a gun."

"And you wanna find out for yourself?" Trapp asked. "That's what a man with your reputation would do, ain't it? Except you're sayin' reputations ain't worth much."

"If I see your men in town I'm going to ask them some questions," Clint said, "not shoot them."

"You ain't law, Adams."

"There's no law here, Trapp," Clint said. "You know what happens then."

"Men make their own."

"That's right," Clint said. "Now remember it."

Clint mounted up and rode off the Boyce ranch.

SEVENTEEN

lint rode back to the river, watched from his saddle as more logs were dropped into the water, then rode over to where the sound of hammering and sawing was still coming from. He saw Tom Allen and Sally, and the big blond waved at him.

"Where's Luke?" he asked, when he rode up to them.

"He'll be here in a minute," Tom said. "You talk to Boyce?"

"I did," Clint said. "It didn't help much. I also talked to his foreman, Trapp."

"How'd that go?" Sally asked.

"Not much better," Clint said.

"Did you tell them about the killing?" Tom asked.

"No," Clint said, "they told me."

"Word got out?" Tom asked.

"How?" Sally asked.

"I don't know," Clint said. "Maybe that's something else we've got to find out."

Luke came over at that point.

"They're almost done here," he said. "We get started tomorrow morning at ten."

"Where are the judges?"

"Should be in town, at the hotel," Tom said. "Why?"

"I want to talk to them."

"The judges?" Luke asked. "What for?"

"Because," Clint said, "I want to talk to everyone who's involved with this."

"What do you think they had to do with killin' Ed?" Tom asked.

"I don't know," Clint said. "That's why I'm going to ask questions."

"We can't go with you," Tom said. "We can't be seen with the judges the night before the competition starts."

"Who's gonna introduce him to the judges?" Sally asked.

"He'll have to introduce himself," Luke said.

"Wait, wait," Clint said, "isn't there a go-between? Somebody linking the judges to the competitors?"

"That would be George Appel," Tom said. "Yeah, George can introduce you."

"Okay," Clint said, "where's George?"

"Where else?" Luke asked.

"The saloon," Sally said.

"Let's get back to town," Clint said.

***

In town they left their horses back at the livery in the care of the hostler, walked over to the saloon. It was late in the day and as they entered, they found the place busier than Clint had ever seen it.

"The night before," Tom said. "Once we get started everybody has to stay sober."

"I get it," Clint said.

They walked to the bar, where they elbowed themselves some room.

"Beer?" Blackie asked.

"Four," Clint said, nodding.

"Comin' up."

When he laid them out Tom asked, "Have you seen George Appel?"

"Sure, he's sittin' in the back with a few of the other boys," Blackie said. "Been there a while."

"Great." Tom looked at Clint. "He's gonna be drunk."

"Well," Clint said, "what do you say we see how drunk?"

They picked up their beers and Clint said to Sally and Luke, "You might as well wait here."

They nodded, and Clint and Tom walked to the back of the room. Tom led him to a table where five brawny men were sitting laughing and slapping their knees, the table top, and each other on the back, spilling more beer than they were drinking.

"The one against the wall is George," Tom said.

The man was large, sweaty, with a mass of red hair and a red beard that was wet, either with beer, spit or both.

"Yep," Clint said, "he looks pretty drunk."

"Well," Tom said, "we won't really know until we talk to him. It takes a lot to get him really drunk." Clint looked at the man again. He looked mighty drunk to him, at the moment.

"Okay," he said. "so let's get him away from his friends and talk to him."

EIGHTEEN

They were able to extricate George Appel from his friend's table, and take him outside onto the boardwalk, into the fresh air.

"George," Tom said, "this is Clint Adams. He's a friend of mine who's—"

"I know who he is," George said. "Adams, good to meet you."

"George," Clint said. "Sorry to take you away from your friends."

"That's okay," George said. "I guess you wanna talk about Ed Fenner?"

"Well," Clint said, "I didn't, but let's do that first. How well did you know Ed?"

The man seemed stone cold sober to Clint, which surprised him. Inside he'd seemed very drunk, but his size—he was at least as big as Tom—probably had something to do with his capacity for liquor.

"I knew him real good," George said. "but before you ask, I don't know who killed him. Oh, and by the way, I didn't kill him."

"Well, somebody did," Clint said, "and they used an axe."

"It wasn't a lumber man," George said.

"Why do you say that?"

"I saw the body," George said. "Those cuts, they

weren't made by anybody who's ever used an axe."

Clint looked at Tom.

"I have to admit," Tom said, "I didn't look at the body that close. I guess I should."

Clint looked back at George.

"When he does," George said, "he'll tell you the same thing. It wasn't one of us."

"Okay," Clint said, "so it was somebody who wanted to make it look like one of you."

"That's what I think."

"It's what I'm thinking, too."

"Oh." The man looked surprised. "Well, good. Uh, you said that wasn't what you wanted to talk to me about. So, what was it?"

"The judges," Clint said. "I want to meet them."

"What for?"

"I need to ask some questions."

"You think one of them may have been involved?"

"I don't know," Clint said, "but I can't satisfy myself that they did or didn't unless I talk to them. And I understand you're the go-between."

"That's right."

"Then I need you to introduce me to them," Clint said.

George looked at Tom, who nodded.

"When?"

"Tonight," Clint said. "Now."

George looked behind him, into the saloon.

"After the introductions you can go back into the saloon and get drunk."

"I am drunk," George said, "but yeah, okay, let's go. They're at the hotel."

"I'll come along," Tom said.

"No, Tom," Clint said, "like you said, you shouldn't

be seen with the judges the night before. Go back inside. I'll come and let you know what happens."

"Okay."

Clint looked at George. "Let's go."

***

In the hotel lobby, Clint suddenly noticed that George was a bit unsteady on his feet.

"You okay?" he asked.

"I told you," George said, with a grin. "I'm drunk, but yeah, I'm okay. Come on let's go up."

Clint followed George to the second floor. He was in room 7, Tom was in 11. George said the judges were in 2, 4, and 15.

"We might as well see the judges in two and four at the same time," he suggested. "Then we can go to the end of the hall and see the one in fifteen."

"That's actually a very good idea," George said.

"Why?"

"You'll see."

They stopped in front of 2 and George knocked. After a moment the door was opened by a tall, but slender man, certainly not a lumberjack.

"Mr. Tompkins? This is Clint Adams. He'd like to talk to the judges."

"About what?" Tompkins asked. He frowned at Clint. "You're not a competitor?"

"No, I'm not."

"Wait," Tompkins said, "I know your name."

As he tried to place it, George stepped down and knocked on the door of room 4. It was opened by a smaller man, pear-shaped, in his fifties, who squinted from behind wire-framed glasses.

"Yes, George?"

"Mr. Strong, this is Clint Adams. He'd like to talk to the judges."

"What?" Strong looked down the hall at the other judge, Tompkins. "Do you know what this is about?"

"No, but I know this fella," Tompkins said. "He's the Gunsmith."

"Why is he here?" Strong asked. Then he looked at Clint. "Why are you here?"

Clint looked at the little man, who was an odd fit for his last name.

"If we could step into one of the rooms, gents," Clint said, "I'll see if I can explain."

Both judges looked at George, who said, "It's kinda important."

"Oh, very well," Tompkins said, "we might as well go into my room."

Strong stepped out of his room, closed the door behind him, and walked down to Tompkins' room.

"Want me to stay?" George asked Clint, as the two judges entered the room.

"No," Clint said, "that's okay. You did what I asked. I'll have one of these judges introduce me to the third. You can head back to the saloon."

"Lemme know if anythin' happens, huh?"

"I'll let you know," Clint said.

NINETEEN

"A logger's been murdered," Clint said, without any warning. He wanted to see their reaction.

"What?" Tompkins said.

Strong's jaw dropped. "The hell, you say!"

"Who?" Tompkins asked.

"A fella named Ed Fenner," Clint said. "I'm told he was a gandy dancer."

"Was he going to be a competitor?" Tompkins asked.

"No," Clint said.

"Well then," Strong said, regaining his composure, "how does this concern us?"

"I don't know that it does," Clint said, "but I thought you should be informed. After all, you're going to be in town for a few days."

"Well, yes," Tompkins said, "then—uh, yes, a warning, then." He looked at his fellow judge. "We should be grateful."

"Of course," Strong said. "We thank you. Are you— is there someone, uh, investigating the matter?"

"There's no law here," Clint said, "so I've been pressed into service to try and find out who did it."

"I see," Tompkins said. "I suppose that makes sense. After all, you are... formidable."

"Yes," Strong said, "formidable."

"Did either of you gents know Ed Fenner?"

"No," Tompkins said, "never heard of him."

"I did not," Strong said.

"Okay, then," Clint said, "I guess we're done here—except I'd like to ask a favor of one of you."

"Oh, yes?" Tompkins said.

"Uh, which one?" Strong asked, looking worried.

"I'd like to be introduced to the third judge," Clint said. "Can one of you do that?"

"Oh, of course," Tompkins said. "You should meet the head judge."

"That's not either of you?" Clint asked.

"Oh, no," Strong said, "neither of us is the head judge."

"I'm curious," Clint said. "Who hired you? Or recruited you? I'm not sure how this works?"

"We were, uh, invited to judge the activities by Mr. Boyce," Tompkins said.

"Ah, so you work for him?"

"No, no," Strong said, "he invited us, and the other competitors had to approve us."

"So everyone agreed on you two as the judges."

"There was a majority agreement," Tompkins said.

"I get you," Clint said. "How about that introduction?"

The two men looked at each other, as if wondering which of them should do it. Finally, they seemed to make a decision.

"I'll take you down there," Strong said. "After all, I have to go back to my own room."

"Fine," Clint said, "I appreciate it." He looked at Tompkins. "Good-night."

"Oh, yes, good-night."

Clint and Strong stepped into the hall.

When they reached the door of room 15, the last room on the floor, Strong seemed to be waiting for Clint to knock, so be obliged. The door was opened almost immediately by a woman with long dark hair, wearing a pair of glasses that she plucked off her nose to take a good look at the two men in the hall.

"Mr. Strong," she said, without looking at him. "Who's your friend?"

"Miss Montero, this is Clint Adams," he said. "He had some news for the judges, which he has already given to Mr. Tompkins and myself."

"I asked Mr. Strong if he'd introduce me to the third judge—the head judge, as I understand it."

"That's right. Clint Adams, is it?"

"It is."

"Are you the famous Clint Adams? The Gunsmith?"

"Right again."

"Well, perhaps you'd better come in, then," she said.

Clint did so, and as Strong started to say something, Miss Montero said, "Thank you, Mr. Strong," and swung the door closed in his face.

The room was warm, and for Clint it was partly because of the woman. She was a tall, dark-skinned beauty, obviously Mexican from her looks if not her name.

"Miss Montero?" he asked.

"Yes," she said, "Marguerite Montero." She extended her hand to him. "A pleasure to meet you."

He shook her hand, found her grip powerful.

"Forgive me for staring," he said. "You're a lovely woman. I can't imagine how you ended up here, as a judge for a competition like this."

"Well, thank you for the compliment," she said. "As

you can tell from my name I'm of Mexican decent, but my parents moved up here when I was young, and they have always been in the lumber business."

"I can't see you wielding an axe, or climbing a tree— or wearing plaid, for that matter."

She laughed. "I climbed many trees as I was growing up. I was a tomboy."

"Now I find that hard to believe."

"Well, I got over it when I... developed," she said. "But I have always known a good lumberjack when I saw one. I started judging when I was young, and eventually became the only female, and certainly the only female head judge."

Clint wondered why Tom and Luke hadn't told him about Marguerite Montero.

TWENTY

"**H**ave a seat, Mr. Adams," she invited.

Clint looked around, saw that they were in a suite. There was a sofa and two chairs in addition to the bed and chest of drawers.

"Quite a room," he said.

"It's the hotel's only suite," she said. "I'm sure they keep it reserved for rich cattleman and such, but the clerk was nice enough to give it to me for the next few days."

"I can't imagine why," Clint said, even though he could. She had probably batted those Mexican black eyes at him.

She sat down on the sofa with her knees together and faced him.

"I have nothing to offer you," she said, and then added, "to drink, I mean."

"That's fine," he said. "I won't be staying long."

"A pity," she said. "So, to what do I owe this visit from the famous Gunsmith?"

"Murder," he said.

"Oh, my," she said. "Do you intend to murder me?"

"Hardly," he said. "There's already been a murder in town. I'm here to inform you about it or, if you prefer, to warn you."

"And who was murdered?"

"A gandy dancer named Ed Fenner."

He used the term, since she had grown up in the business. Her expression grew grave.

"I knew Ed," she said. "He was very good at his job. I'm sure whoever won the Boyce contract would have hired him."

"That's what I've heard," he said. "As someone who knew him, can you think of any reason someone would want to kill him?"

"No, I can't say I do. But... there's no sheriff or marshal here. Are you..."

"I'm investigating his murder," Clint said. "There's just no one else to do it."

"I see," she said. "And how was he killed?"

"With an axe."

She closed her eyes and shuddered, then opened them.

"I'm so sorry," she said. "I suppose since an axe was used you suspect a lumber man?"

"Not necessarily," he said. "I'm told the cuts were not what an expert with an axe would leave behind."

"I see," she said, "then someone wants it to look like another lumber man killed him."

"That's possible."

"Are we going on with the competition?"

"Tomorrow, as planned," he said. "Ten a.m.?"

"That's what I was told."

He stood up. "Then I'll leave you to get your rest so you can get up in the morning and have a good breakfast."

She rose and said, "I appreciate that."

She walked him to the door.

"Please," she said, "if there's anything else you think I can do to help, let me know."

"I will," he said. "Oh, do you know if Ed had a wife?"

"He didn't," she said. "Unless he got married since the last time I saw him."

"And when was that?"

"Last month, in Juno."

"Alaska?"

She nodded.

"I was a judge there, and he was looking for work."

"Did he find it?"

"I—I don't know," she said. "I left after the competition, and didn't see him again. And now... I guess I never will."

"Were you good friends?"

"No," she said, "he was just a nice man. Always very respectful, not..."

"Not what?"

"Like a lot of the other men," she said. "Not everyone likes having a female judge. And lumberjacks are not generally known for being gentlemen."

"Why do you stay around them, then?"

She smiled. "Do you think it would different around other men? Cattlemen, for instance?"

"Not likely."

"Well, there you are," she said. "And this is the business I grew up around."

They stood there by the door awkwardly for a moment, and then she opened it for him.

"I'll say good-night, then."

"Thank you for the... warning," she said.

"Sure."

He stepped into the hall.

"Will I see you tomorrow, at the competition?"

"Oh yes," he said, "I'll be there rooting on my friend, Tom Allen."

"Oh!" She seemed surprised. "You didn't say that

you and Tom were friends."

"Didn't I?" he asked. "I guess I didn't think it mattered. Do you know Tom?"

"I know most of the men who will be competing tomorrow, Mr. Adams."

"Clint," he said, "call me Clint."

"All right, Clint," she said, "and I would like it very much if you called me Marguerite."

"Then I will," he said, "Marguerite."

She put her hand out again and he took it.

"Good-night," she said.

"Good-night."

He turned and walked down the hall. He didn't hear the door close until he had reached the front of the hall and started walking down the stairs.

TWENTY-ONE

When Clint got down to the lobby he looked at the desk clerk, who seemed to be very nervous. He couldn't keep his hands still, and his eyes were shifting about, looking everywhere but at Clint.

Clint approached the desk. "You're name's Terry, isn't it?"

"Huh? Oh, uh, yes sir," the clerk said, after swallowing and moistening his lips.

"What's making you so nervous, Terry?"

"Huh? Nervous?" Terry asked, his voice almost a squeak. "I ain't, uh, nervo—"

"Is there somebody out front waiting for me, Terry?" Clint asked.

"Well, uh—"

"They came in, asked if I was here?" Clint said. "You told them I was, so they decided to wait out front?"

Terry stared at Clint with his mouth open, then asked, "How did you know that?"

"Don't worry about it," Clint said. "All you need to do now is tell me who it is."

"Oh, it's, uh, some men from the Boyce ranch."

"How many?"

"Uh—"

"Let me guess," Clint said. "Five?"

Terry's mouth opened again.

"Just a good guess," Clint said, thinking about Boyce's men Titleman, Jensen, and their three friends. "Are any of them out back?"

"No, sir," Terry said. "They're all out front, waitin'."

"Are you sure?"

The clerk squared his shoulders and said, "I'm positive, sir."

"Okay, then," Clint said. "Good man, Terry. I'll go out the back and leave them waiting out front. After a while they'll get impatient and come back in."

"They will?" Terry didn't like that idea.

"Yes, they will," Clint said. "You tell them you haven't seen me come down."

"Uh, okay."

"If they want my room number, go ahead and give it to them. Don't worry about it."

"Okay."

Clint gave the clerk a couple of dollars.

"Relax," Clint said. "Take some deep breaths. Don't show them how nervous you are."

"Yessir! Thank you."

Clint had seen the back door the day he and Tom had taken their baths, so he went down the hall and out of the hotel that way. He thought about going around front and surprising the five men, but it was getting dark, and for any kind of firefight in the street he preferred sunlight.

Let them get impatient, and frustrated.

He made his way over to the saloon.

***

He found Tom, Luke and Sally standing at the bar, each working on a beer.

"Is George here?" he asked.

"He's in the back again," Tom said. "Havin' a good time."

"You met the judges?" Luke asked.

"I did."

"All three?"

"All three of them."

"Even Marguerite?" Tom asked, he and Luke grinning at each other.

"Yes, even Miss Montero."

"Marguerite?" Sally said. "That bitch is in town?"

"She's the head judge," Tom said.

"Oh, Christ," Sally said. "There goes any chance I had of winnin'."

"You and Miss Montero have problems?" Clint asked.

"That bitch!" Sally spat, but that was all she offered. She went back to her beer.

"She seemed pretty nice to me," Clint said.

"Marguerite is all right," Tom said. "Don't pay any attention to Sally."

Sally made a sound with her mouth and pushed her empty mug toward Blackie, who gave her another.

"Anythin' that means <u>anythin'</u> happen?" Tom asked.

"No," Clint said. "The judges all seemed surprised about Ed's murder. None of them had anything to offer."

"So we haven't gotten anywhere," Tom said.

"No," Clint said, "We have no real suspects, and we really can't eliminate anyone."

"Why can't you eliminate loggers?" Luke asked. "I mean, the sloppy work with the axe—"

"—could be deliberate," Clint said. "Could be the work of a logger who wanted it to look like it wasn't a logger."

Luke shook his head. "That's... confusin'."

"Yeah, it is," Clint said, "but it still means I can't eliminate anybody."

"Well," Luke said, "except us."

"Yes," Clint said, "except for you two... maybe."

"And me," Sally said. "I didn't kill him."

"Okay," Clint said, "you three."

"And you," Tom said.

"I didn't know him," Clint said. "I'm not in the mix."

"Beer?" Blackie asked him.

"Yes."

When Clint had his beer, he pulled Tom to one side, away from Luke and Sally, who were talking between themselves.

"Is there a cathouse in town?" he asked.

"Why?" Tom asked. "Sally not enough for you?"

"I'm wondering," Clint said, ignoring the remark, "what the lumberjacks do for female company. The cowboys have some girls over at their saloon."

"Yeah, they do," Tom said, "including Boyce's daughter."

"So I heard," Clint said. "Does she just serve drinks, or does she take men upstairs?"

"I don't know," Tom said. "I haven't been over there for that. And no, there's not a cathouse... well, not really."

"What's that mean?" Clint asked. "Not really?"

"Drink your beer," Tom said, "and I'll show you."

***

"What's going on?" Jensen asked Frank Titleman. "Is he comin' out or what?"

"It's a little early for anybody to be turnin' in, right now," Titleman said. "I mean, he's old, but the Gunsmith ain't that old."

"Then where is he?" Jensen asked.

Titleman turned to the other three men, lounging behind them on the boardwalk across from the hotel.

"A couple of you guys go inside and find out if the Gunsmith is still in there."

"How do we do that?" Andy Culver said.

"Try askin' the desk clerk," Titleman said.

"And what if he don't know?" Phil Vincent asked.

"Then go upstairs and check his room," Titleman said. "I wanna know if we're standin' out here with our peters in our hands. Now move!"

TWENTY-TWO

efore they left the saloon, Clint put his hand on Tom's arm to stop him.

"I just remembered," he said. "There were some men looking for me at the hotel. I think it was that fella Frank Titleman and his friends."

"And what's that about?" Tom asked. "Didn't Boyce cooperate with you?"

"He did, but apparently Titleman has a mind of his own," Clint said.

"Well, from what I hear he does fancy himself fast with a gun," Tom said. "Maybe he just wants to try you."

"I don't need that kind of nonsense right now," Clint said. "Is there a back way out of here?"

"Yeah, there is," Tom said, "but isn't that gonna make you look bad? I mean, with your rep, you can't be walkin' away from a fight, can you?"

"I'm not walkin' away from a fight," Clint said, "I'm allowing Titleman and his friends to stay alive."

"What if he and his friends aren't even out there?"

"That's okay, too," Clint said, "but let's play it this way, for now."

"Whatever you say."

***

"You sure this is gonna work?" Hank Jensen asked his friend, Frank Titleman.

They were standing across the street from the hotel.

"The Gunsmith ain't at the hotel, is he?" Titleman asked.

"Well, no, but—"

"So where else can he be?"

"Well—"

"In the saloon, with his lumberjack friends, that's where," Titleman said. "And we're gonna wait right here until he comes out."

"But..."

"But what?"

Jensen leaned in so the other three wouldn't hear. Once again, Vincent, Culver and the other man, Hunter, were standing behind them, waiting.

"What're we gonna do, face him in the street?" Jensen said. "I mean, he's the Gunsmith."

"I know who he is, Jensen," Titleman said. "You let me worry about that."

"Frank," Jensen said, "are you sure you can take him?"

Titleman looked Jensen right in the eyes.

"Hank," he said, "I just told you to let me worry about it. What part of that don't you understand?"

"Yeah, okay, Frank. Okay."

Jensen walked over and joined the other four men, leaving Titleman standing alone in the street.

***

Tom walked Clint to one end of town, where a large, two story building stood.

"Two sisters own this building," Tom said. "They say

they're going to open a boutique in town—whatever that is."

"A woman's clothing store."

"Oh," Tom said, "well, before they can do that they said they needed to make some money, so..."

"So they entertain men?" Clint asked.

"They've been known to," Tom said, "but they're not a full blown whorehouse. They don't want to be known in town as whores. They figure before the town fully gets up and running—with a Mayor, a sheriff, a town council—they'll stop what they're doing, and open their store."

"So... they might have entertained the man who killed Ed Fenner."

"Yeah, I guess."

"Do you know them?" Clint asked. "I mean, obviously you do, since you know their story—"

"That's only because I built the house."

"Do you think you can get them to talk to me?"

"I don't know," Tom said, "I could try. When?"

"Well," Clint said, "we're here..."

***

They were the Briscoe sisters, Ann and Lucy.

One of them opened the door to Tom's knock and greeted him with a warm smile.

"Hello, Tom," she said. "So nice to see you."

"Hello, Lucy."

"Who's your friend?"

"This is Clint Adams," Tom said. "He'd like to talk to you and Ann."

"Really?" she asked. "Talk?"

"Just talk," Clint said.

"Well then," she said, "perhaps you gentlemen should come in."

They followed her and found the other Briscoe sister waiting in a sitting room. Tom hadn't told Clint that they were twins. Both were medium height, brunette, very pretty but—surprisingly,--young, no more than mid-twenties.

"Ann, Tom has brought a friend to talk to us."

"Talk?" Ann asked.

"Just talk, apparently," Lucy said. "This is Mister Clint Adams."

"Oh," Ann said, "the Gunsmith."

Both were wearing plain cotton shirts, Lucy blue, Ann green. Neither was dressed the way a whore would be to entertain men.

"Oh!" Lucy said, "Really? I didn't recognize the name. I'm so stupid."

"I'm sure you're not," Clint said.

"Can I make us some tea?" Ann said.

"Not for me," Clint said. "I just have a question or two, so we won't keep you two ladies very long."

"Let's all sit down, then," Lucy said.

The sisters sat next to each other on the sofa, and it was very disconcerting to see them there. Clint sat in one armchair, Tom in the other.

"What's this about?" Lucy asked.

"Tom told me about you're, uh, sideline," Clint said.

"I hope you don't think badly of us," Ann said. "It's just a way to an end for us."

"I'm not here to judge. I mean, who am I to do that? No, I just have some questions about something that happened here in town."

"The murder?" Lucy asked.

"Word has gotten around," Tom said.

"But we don't know who was murdered," Ann told them.

"A man named Ed Fenner," Clint said.

"Oh, Mr. Fenner," Lucy said. "What a nice man."

"He's been here?" Clint asked.

"Once or twice," Ann said.

"Well, I don't need to know him," Clint said, "I need to know if any other men may have come here who might have mentioned Ed. Maybe been looking for him?"

"You think his killer may have been here?" Lucy asked.

"How gruesome," Ann said.

"I'm sure if such a man was here," Lucy said, "he certainly wouldn't have talked about killing Mr. Fenner."

"No, but if he was a stranger here he might have mentioned that he was looking for him."

"Why would a stranger be looking for him?" Ann asked.

"He might have been hired to kill him."

"Of course," Ann said. "There I go, being stupid again. Lucy is the one with the brains."

Nobody said anything to that.

"We haven't entertained any strangers this week, Mr. Adams," Lucy said. "I'm sorry if that's not helpful to you."

"Don't be sorry," Clint said. "I'm just trying to make sure I'm thorough. Have you had anyone here—whether a lumber man or a cowhand—who might have mentioned having a beef with Ed Fenner?"

Ann looked at her sister, leaving it to her to answer the question.

"I can't say that we have," Lucy said.

"We're not being very helpful, are we?" Ann said.

Clint stood up. "You've been very helpful. Those

were just questions I felt needed to be answered."

Both women stood and Lucy said, "Well then, Ann will show you out."

***

During the walk to the door, Ann linked her arm in Clint's left one.

"How long will you be in town?" she asked.

"Until the lumberjack competition is over and someone has won the Boyce contract," he said.

"Well," she said, linking her other arm in Tom's, "that should be Tom, here."

"We hope so," Tom said.

She opened the front door for them. Tom went out first, and as Clint started out she grabbed a handful of his shirt.

"Stop in and see us again, Clint," she said. "That is, stop in and see me again. Like I said, Lucy's the brains." Her inference was clear. She was the physical side of the sisterhood.

"I'll keep that in mind," he promised.

"You do that."

He stepped out and she closed the door.

They went down the walk and stopped at the end, turning around to look at the house again.

"What an interesting pair," Clint said.

"To say the least," Tom agreed. "But still no help."

"Nope," Clint said, "nobody's supplying very much help, are they?"

"It's not like they ain't tryin', Clint."

"Maybe," Clint said. "Maybe."

TWENTY-THREE

They went back towards the saloon, stopped just down the street so they could take a look. There were no street lamps throughout the new town yet, but there were several right in front of the two saloons. By that light they were able to see a man standing in the street, and four figures behind him.

"Yep," Tom said, "there they are."

"They got tired of waiting outside the hotel," Clint said, "and they're going to get tired of waiting outside the saloon."

"You think they're gonna come in?"

"With the place loaded with lumberjacks?" Clint said. "I doubt it." He slapped Tom on the back. "Come on, we'll go back in the rear door. Let them get good and frustrated."

They ducked down and alley to the back of the saloon.

***

They spent the rest of the evening there, with Luke and Sally. They told them where they had just been and what they had found out.

"Nothing," Clint said.

"Those twins?" Sally said. "You went to them?"

"Just to see if they'd heard anything," Clint said.

"Oh, they've heard things, all right," she said. "Grunt and groans from the men who pay them."

"Well, I was hoping that in between those grunts and groans they might have heard a name or two of someone who had something against Ed Fenner."

"There was nothin'," Tom said.

"So far all I've run up against are dead ends," Clint said.

"So what's next?" Luke asked.

"If I had access to a telegraph key I'd send for help."

"From who?" Sally asked.

"I have a friend named Talbot Roper," Clint said. "He's the best private detective in the country, works out of Denver. I'd ask him for help. But there's no key here."

"The nearest one's in Cascade," Luke said.

"That's a long way off," Sally said.

"We could send somebody with the message," Tom said. "How long would it take Mr. Roper to get here?"

"Well, he'd come by rail," Clint said. "Two days, probably, but he'd have to be in Denver when the telegram gets there."

"By the time he gets here the competition might be over," Tom said. "And nobody's gonna leave here until then."

"So your suspects will still be here," Luke said.

"Unless," Clint said, "Ed was killed by a stranger, who has come and gone, already."

"In which case," Tom said, "you'll never catch him."

"Right."

"Is that acceptable?" Sally asked.

"He was your friend," Clint said, looking at the three of them. "You tell me."

"It's not to me," Luke said. "I'd like to know who

98

killed Ed."

"So would I," Sally said.

Tom looked at Clint and nodded.

"All right, then," Clint said, "let's just assume that the killer is still here and take it from there."

"So, are we sending someone to Cascade to contact your friend?" Tom asked.

"We could," Clint said. "Do you have someone who's not competing tomorrow, and who can ride?"

Tom and Luke both turned to look out over the sea of lumberjacks that now inhabited the saloon.

"Hey," Blackie said to Clint and Sally, "I think I came up with a name for this place."

"Really?" Sally asked.

"What is it?" Clint asked.

"Blackie's." He looked very happy. "Blackie's Saloon. Whataya think?"

"I think it's brilliant," Sally said.

"Genius," Clint said.

"I'm gonna have a sign made up tomorrow mornin'," he said. "By tomorrow night it'll be hangin' over the front entrance."

"That's great," Sally said. "That calls for a free beer."

"It sure does," Blackie said.

"For all four of us," she said.

"Uh, yeah, sure."

Clint looked at Tom and Luke.

"How about Hagan?" Luke asked.

"He rides a mule," Tom said. "It'd take him forever to get to Cascade."

"You're right."

"How about Sark? He's got a good horse."

"Sark would fall off his horse before he got out of town," Luke said.

"That's true. But we could use his horse."

"All we need," Luke said, "is somebody who could ride it."

"Somebody trustworthy," Clint added.

Tom and Luke looked at each other, then at their fresh, free beers on the bar.

"Keep thinking," Clint said. "Come up with somebody by morning."

Luke picked up his beer and said, "This will be thirsty work."

TWENTY-FOUR

lint woke the next morning with Sally down between his legs.

"I have to get going," she said, nuzzling his semi-erect cock. "I'll need some breakfast if I'm gonna compete at full energy."

As he grew harder he said, "You seem to be at full energy right now."

"Nu-uh," she said, "you do." She opened her mouth and took him inside. She sucked him, sliding her lips up and down the length of him, wetting him, massaging his balls, and she kept at it until he had to lift his hips up off the bed just before exploding into her mouth.

***

He watched her get dressed a short time later.

"I could come to breakfast with you."

"No," she said, "they lay out a meal for all the competitors. Nobody else is invited. That's when they go over all the rules."

"Fine," he said, "I'll get my own breakfast."

She smiled and, at the door, blew him a kiss.

"I'll see you out there."

"Good luck!" he said.

***

Tom Allen flipped Ann Briscoe over onto her back, spread her long, slender legs and drove himself into the hot, wet depths of her pussy.

"Oh yeah!" she growled at him. "Come on, Tom, harder."

"You don't fool me, Ann."

"Why would I try to fool you, love?"

"When I came to the door," he said, driving himself into her harder and harder, "you were hoping I was the Gunsmith."

She laughed. "Well, I've never been with a legend, have I?"

"And maybe you never will," Tom, said, "so you might as well enjoy this."

"Oh, I am, darling," she said.

From down the hall Ann heard her sister scream.

"And it sounds like Lucy is enjoying your friend Luke."

"Luke," he said, "has a certain body part size in common with a bull."

"I know," she said. "My sister likes that."

Lucy screamed again.

"Sounds like she's goin' a little overboard," Tom said.

"Well," Ann said, with a grin, "let's try and go a little overboard ourselves, shall we?"

He laughed and grabbed her ankles, spreading her legs wide.

Ann screamed, a sound she knew echoed down the hall to her sister's room.

***

Luke met Tom at the front door.

"We gotta get to that breakfast," he said.

"I know," Tom said, "but we've got to talk to Clint first, tell him we got a rider for him."

"We better hurry, then."

As they went out the door Tom said, "Man, but Lucy can scream real loud."

"What about Ann?" Luke asked. "She did her part."

"I don't think either of them girls are gonna be walkin' straight today," Tom said.

Luke slapped him on the back, laughing.

***

Upstairs Lucy came down the hall to Ann's room, as she was putting the finishing touches to her hair.

"Ready for breakfast?" Lucy asked.

"Definitely, if you're cookin'."

"Do you ever cook?"

"No."

"Then I'm cookin'," Lucy said.

As they went down the stairs Lucy said, "My throat hurts."

"Well," Ann said, "you did overdo it a bit."

"That Luke is built like a bull," Lucy said. "I was only half puttin' it on."

"It was that good?"

"It was that hard," Lucy said. "I didn't say it was that good."

In the kitchen, Ann sat at the table while Lucy put the coffee on and then started to cook breakfast.

"What do you think about this murder?" Ann asked.

"I think we should mind our own business," Lucy said.

"But we do know somethin'."

"We don't know who killed Fenner," Lucy said. "Not for sure."

"But we could get Clint Adams to come back," Ann said, with a smile. "That would be excitin'."

"Forget it, Ann," Lucy said. "That would be playing with fire."

"I like playin' with fire."

"I don't," Lucy said. "Let's just keep to ourselves on this."

Ann made a face.

***

Clint was on his way to the little café for breakfast when he saw the two loggers coming toward him.

"Don't you guys have someplace to be?" he asked.

"Yeah, we're on our way," Tom said, "but we wanted to tell you we got you a rider."

"Who?"

"His name's Dave Cabrera," Tom said. "We figured you'd be havin' breakfast at the café, so we told him to meet you there this mornin'."

"That's good," Clint said. "And he's reliable?"

"We both agree, he is," Tom said, and Luke nodded.

"Okay, then," Clint said. "I appreciate it."

"You get your detective friend out here," Luke said. "Between the two of you, you'll find out who killed Ed."

"I hope you're right."

Tom said, "See you out there later," and the two loggers ran off.

TWENTY-FIVE

lint was in the middle of his breakfast when a man entered the café and looked around. Only a couple of the other tables were taken, so he quickly made his decision and approached Clint.

"Clint Adams?" he asked.

"That's right."

"I'm Dave Cabrera."

"Have a seat, Dave."

The man pulled out the chair across from Clint and sat. He was a sad looking man in his forties, seemed to be all arms and legs.

"Coffee?"

"Thanks."

Clint filled a cup for the man and pushed it over to him.

"Did Tom tell you what I need?"

"You need somebody who can ride," Cabrera said.

"That's right."

"I been riding since I was six."

"What are you doing up here?" Clint asked.

"Well, I'm not a lumberjack, if that's what you're wonderin'," Cabrera said. "I, uh, had some trouble with the law down South, so I came up here to start over. Seems like I found me a new town."

"Have you been to Cascade?"

"I have."

"And is there a telegraph office there?"

"Yeah."

"And a lawman?"

"A sheriff."

Clint thought a moment.

"Is Cascade in the same county as this town?" he then asked.

"Naw, it ain't."

"So the sheriff of Cascade wouldn't come here," Clint said.

"It would be out of his jurisdiction," Cabrera said.

"Okay, then," Clint said, "I guess I'll stick to my original plan. I need you to send a telegram for me."

"I can do that."

"Do you want to know to who, and where?"

"Am I gettin' paid for this job?"

"You are."

"Then I don't need to know who or where," Cabrera said. "Just tell me what I'm gettin' paid to do."

"Finish your coffee," Clint said, taking out a pencil and paper he'd gotten from the hotel clerk, "while I write out my telegram."

"Sure."

"He noticed Cabrera eyeing the last piece of bacon on his plate, and said, "And help yourself to whatever's left here. Unless you want a plate for yourself?"

"We got time?"

"Sure, we've got time," Clint said. "I'll need you to have the energy to make this ride."

"Yes, sir!"

Clint waved the waiter over and said, "Bring Mr. Cabrera anything he wants."

"Yes, sir."

Clint started to write.

***

After Cabrera finished his breakfast, Clint walked him over to the livery stable. He wanted to get a look at the man's horse. It was a fine looking five or six year old roan, and since the ride was only fifty miles, Clint was sure the man's animal was capable of making the trip.

Cabrera mounted up with Clint's telegram folded into his shirt pocket.

"Don't stop for anything," he told Cabrera. "I don't care what you see on the trail."

"And you want me to wait for a reply, right?"

"Right," Clint said. If Roper wasn't in his office, there should be someone there to send a reply. "But as soon as you get it, you ride back here. Don't stop for a drink, if you want to have a meal have it while you're waiting. And if it gets dark along the way, go ahead and camp. I don't want you to break your neck riding at night. But I fully expect you back here day after tomorrow."

"That shouldn't be a problem, Mr. Adams."

"And then you'll get the second half of your payment." He'd given Cabrera the first half while they were still in the café.

"I understand."

"Now get going." He slapped the roan on the butt, and the animal leaped forward into a run.

TWENTY-SIX

With Cabrera on the way to Cascade to send the telegram to Roper, Clint saddled Eclipse and rode out
to where the competition was being held. When he
arrived he saw an area for horses to be picketed, and bug-
gies and buckboards to be parked. He left Eclipse with
the other animals, but not tied as they were.

Because the town was so new, there weren't that
many spectators for the contest. Most of the people
were competitors—except for the three judges who were
seated on an elevated stand, so they'd be able to observe
from a higher vantage point.

The spectators were competitors who were not involved in the event currently being conducted, plus a few
people from town. They were standing behind a rope,
which kept them off the field of competition. Clint joined
them there.

"What's going on?" Clint asked a man, as he moved
in next to him.

"This is a pretty simple one," the man said. "It's
just climbing to the top of the tree, and then back down
again. First one back on the ground wins and goes on to
the next round."

"How many rounds are there?"

"Depends on how many competitors there are," the
man said. "They go three at a time. I think there's twelve

of them competing in this event, so that'd be four heats."

"That would leave four competitors for the last heat, wouldn't it?"

"They'll probably go two and two, and the last two will compete in the finale."

"This could take a while," Clint said. "Can't they hold another event at the same time?"

"Kinda hard with only three judges," the man said, "but they will do that later. Some of the events on the lake will be held at the same time, and the judges will split up."

"Thanks for filling me in."

The man looked at him for the first time.

"Never been to one of these before?" he asked.

"No, this is my first."

"My name's Ted Shelton," the man said.

"Clint," Clint said, and they shook hands.

"You got any more questions, feel free to ask."

"I assume you've been to many of these?"

"Watched a lot, competed in a lot."

"Not competing today?"

"Naw," he said, "my competing days are done. I'll just try to get hired by whoever wins."

Ted looked to be in his 30's, a small, wiry man. He seemed too young to have stopped competing, but when Clint saw him move, there appeared to be something wrong with one foot or leg. He decided not to ask about it. He'd confine any questions to the events.

As he watched he saw that Tom, Luke and Sally were competing in this event, but that they weren't going against each other in these first rounds.

Tom went first. Each competitor had a belt that they looped around the tree, and would use to climb up and down. Clint was amazed at the speed with which Tom manipulated the belt, climbed to the top, and then descended, being the first one to touch the ground, winning his heat.

"That's no surprise," Shelton said. "Tom Allen should win a lot of these events."

"And the contract?"

"Maybe."

"Who's the competition?"

"See that man at the center tree?"

Clint looked. A big, beefy man was looping his belt around the same tree Tom had used. He was about Tom's age, heavier through the shoulders and—judging by the tree itself—about the same height.

"That's Clyde Norton," Ted Shelton said. "He's Allen's biggest competition for the job."

"He looks too heavy for this event."

"Watch him."

Clint did. When the starter said go, Clyde Norton was up and down the tree twice as fast as either of his competitors, winning his heat.

"That was faster than Allen," Shelton said.

"Are you sure?"

"Oh, yeah."

"So when they go head-to-head—"

"—Tom Allen is gonna have to go a lot faster."

The third heat included Luke, who came in second, and the fourth heat had Sally in it. She won.

Luke was out.

Tom came over to where Clint was standing next to Ted Shelton.

"Hey, Clint."

"You did well," Clint said.

"Did you see Clyde? He was the one—"

"Yeah, Ted told me."

111

"Hi, Ted."

"Tom. This here a friend of yours?"

"Yeah, he is."

"Glad I didn't say anythin' wrong."

"Ted's been real helpful."

"'scuse us, Ted." Tom took Clint's arm and moved him away from the other man. "You get Dave off okay?"

"He's on his way."

"Good," Clint said.

"Who are you going against next?"

"Sally's gotta go against Clyde," Tom said. "I'm paired with Zeke Tyler. He's a good man, but I'll beat him."

"And Sally?"

Tom shook his head.

"She's got no chance."

"So it'll be you and Clyde."

"Yeah."

"Ted says he's your biggest competition for the contract."

"He is," Tom said, "and he's already got a crew. If I needed a big job done, I'd hire him."

"That's quite an endorsement."

"Yeah, but I've got to beat him," Tom said. "I need this job."

"There goes Sally." Clint pointed.

Tom turned and they watched Sally loop her belt around one of the trees. Clyde came up next to her and said something, then laughed and walked to another tree. The look on Sally's face said it all. She wanted Clyde to climb to the top, and then fall off.

"This is gonna be brutal," Tom said.

"She's got no chance?" Clint asked.

"No, chance," Tom said. "He just got inside her head."

When the starter fired the pistol for them to go, Sally's right foot immediately slipped, and it was all over. Clyde was waiting for her at the bottom when she got down. He said something to her again, and she turned and swung at him. He backed away, laughing as she stumbled from the miss.

Tom ran over and grabbed Sally before she could go after Clyde, and sent her to Clint.

"That sonofabitch!" she swore. "I'll kill him."

"You can't let him get to you, Sally," Clint said.

"I can't stop him!" she swore.

"Why not?"

She turned to look at Clint, her face stormy, her arms folded across her chest.

"We have a history."

"Ah," Clint said.

"Yeah," she said, "that explains it all, right?"

"There goes Tom," he said.

"Tom'll beat Zeke easy."

"And what about Clyde?"

She looked worried.

"I don't know," she said. "Clyde's a helluva climber, and a chopper. But Tom's a better log roller. On the river Tom's a better man."

"But on land?"

"He's gotta try harder," she said.

"Well," Clint said, "let's watch and see."

When the starter sent them on their way it was clear Tom was going to beat Zeke Tyler. He got to the bottom before Tyler, but not that far ahead of him.

"Jesus," Sally said.

"What?"

"Tom's not gonna beat Clyde that way," she said. "That was too slow."

"Maybe he just went as fast as he had to," Clint suggested, "to beat Tyler."

"Maybe," she said, biting her lip. "I need Tom to win this contract, Clint. I need the work, and I won't work for Clyde if he wins it."

"We'll just have to wait and see," Clint said, "and hope."

"Or," she said, "you could shoot Clyde in the foot, accidental
like."

He hoped she was kidding.

TWENTY-SEVEN

hey gave Tom and Clyde a short break before they had to face off against each other.

"I need this one," Tom said to Clint, Luke and Sally. "It would really be good for me to start out winnin'."

"Don't let him get inside your head," Sally said.

"He can't get in my head," Tom said. "He's got nothin' on me."

"Then you get to him," Luke suggested.

"How do you suggest I do that?" Tom asked.

Clint and Luke looked at Sally.

"Okay, use me," she said.

"You and Clyde?"

"Once upon a time," she said, "until I got tired of him."

"I'm sure he'll be glad to hear that," Tom said.

"Try it," Clint said. "Who knows? All you need is a split second advantage."

Tom looked over to where Clyde was already looping his belt around the tree trunk.

"Okay," Tom said, rubbing his hands together, "I'll give it my best try."

He walked over to a tree with his belt, looped it around, then leaned over and said something to Clyde Norton that seemed to annoy the man.

When the starter fired his gun it actually looked like Tom got that split second advantage he needed. Both men went up the tree at amazing speed, touched the top and then started back down again. There was not even a difference in their heights to aid one of them in touching his feet to the ground first. It looked dead even to Clint as they reached the ground, and the decision actually had to go to the judges.

In the end, they decided that Tom Allen had touched the ground first.

Tom happily came over to Clint, Luke and Sally and accepted hugs and slaps on the back.

Clyde approached them, a deep frown on his face.

"That's how you wanna play it, huh, Allen?" he asked.

"Hey," Tom said, "all's fair, Clyde."

"What about what you did to me?" Sally demanded.

Clyde looked at her and said, "Ah, you're just too easy, Sally."

"Sonofabitch—" she said, and would have attacked him if Clint hadn't grabbed her.

"You better go, Clyde," Tom said.

"Yeah," Luke said, "you better practice."

"I don't need practice to beat you," Clyde said to Allen. "I'll see you with the axe."

Clint looked at Tom.

"With an axe?"

"The axe throwing event," Tom said. "He's pretty good."

"And you?"

Tom grinned. "I'm better."

"Not better than me," Luke said. "This is my best event."

"I don't care if you win, or I win," Tom said, "I just

don't want Clyde to win."

Clint looked at Sally. "And what about you?"

"Throwin' an axe is not ladylike," she admonished him.

"Sorry."

***

When the judges took a break, Clint walked over to where Marguerite Montero was standing.

"Miss Montero."

"Mr. Adams," she said. "I saw you standing on the sidelines. Are you rooting for your blonde friend?"

"Sally?" Clint asked. "Yeah, I'm rooting for her, along with Luke and Tom."

"Tom Allen has a good chance of winning this," she said. "I don't know about the other two. Also, Clyde Norton."

"Judges are supposed to be impartial, aren't they?" he asked.

"Oh, we are," she said, "but we recognize who has the most talent. Even so, it all depends on who performs the best at that moment. It must be the same for you."

"For me?"

"In events that you compete in," she said. "Um, shooting targets? Have you done that?"

"Once or twice."

"And there are judges, right?"

"That's right."

"There you are," she said. "I'm sure they recognize you as the best, but you also have to be the best on that day."

"It's true enough."

"Marguerite?" one of the other judges called.

"I've got to go," she said. "I'll see you later... perhaps."

He watched her ascended the judges platform and seat herself between the two male judges, then went back to the sidelines to watch the axe throwing competition.

***

Sally stood next to him as the competitors lined up. In addition to Luke, Tom and Clyde, there were eight others, but in quick order the contest dwindled down to Tom, Luke and Clyde.

Clint found it interesting that the axe throwing competitors used a pretty typical bullseye type target, painted into a large wooden background.

He could also see why Sally wasn't involved. The axe that they were throwing was large, heavy, and took two hands to throw.

Both Luke and Clyde were heavier through the shoulders and chest than Tom, and while those men seemed to toss the axe with more power, Tom's advantage seemed to be in his accuracy.

Yet even when the contest got down to the three of them, they had to toss more than once before the judges could decide on the final two contestants.

One of the judges—the smaller one with the glasses—stood and announced, "The two contestants who will toss for the win are Big Luke Connors and Clyde Norton!"

Unhappily, Tom stalked over to the where Clint and Sally were standing.

"Is this going to hurt your chances?" Clint asked.

"Only if Clyde wins," Tom said. "Luke's gotta beat him."

"He will," Sally said. "Just watch."

***

After three throws, the two men were inseparable. The judges put their heads together, and decided that the competitors should back up another ten feet, and throw a fourth time.

Clyde threw first. He reared back with both hands, hefting the axe over his head, and let it fly. It turned end-over-end several times as it flew towards the target, then struck with a loud THWACK.

"That looks good," Sally said, sadly.

The taller male judge approached the target, examined it, then backed away. The axe was removed, and it was up to Luke to throw.

He hefted his axe over his head and let it go. Clint felt Tom Allen tense next to him, and felt Sally's hands dig into his arm as the axe flew toward the target and then bit into it loudly.

The judge stepped forward, examined the axe, then rejoined the other two judges on the stand.

It was Marguerite, the head judge, who stood up, stepped forward and announced, "The winner is... Big Luke Connors!"

TWENTY-EIGHT

"Tell me about Clyde Norton," Clint said to Tom Allen, during a break in the action.

"He's a good worker," Tom said, "put together his own crew last year and has been getting lots of jobs."

"Seems to me—judging just from what I've seen today—that he's a man who will do whatever he has to do to get the job done."

"It's true," Tom said, "but I think that pretty much describes most of us."

"He seems to have a knack for getting inside people's heads," Clint commented.

"Naw, that's just Sally," Tom said. "He and Sally used to be together, but it didn't last long."

"Why not?"

"He doesn't know how to treat a lady—not that Sally's a lady, but she's a woman, and he doesn't know how to treat them, either."

"What makes you say she's not a lady?"

"Don't get all defensive," Tom said, "she says it herself that she's not all girlie."

Clint knew that, very well. He looked around, spotted her off to the side, holding a saw.

"How does the sawing work?" Clint asked.

"We have two man sawing competitions, and then one man," Tom said. "Then there's the chopping."

121

"And after that?"

"After that we go down to the river."

"Who's your partner in the two man sawing event?"

"Who else?" Tom said, with a grin. "Big Luke. We should win that one, easy."

"And the one man?"

"Clyde's hard to beat, there."

"This competition sounds like it's going to be tight," Clint said. "Is there anybody else here you're afraid of?"

"Naw, just Clyde," Tom said. "I mean, if Luke had his own crew, then I'd be worried about him."

"He seems pretty loyal to you," Clint said. "What's that about?"

"He's a little younger than I am," Tom said. "I think it's kind of a big brother thing."

"Well, I'd rather have him on my side than against me," Clint said.

"I agree with you, there."

Clint was about to say something else when Tom looked past him and frowned.

"Now what are they doin' here?"

Clint turned and saw a crowd of men approaching. They looked like cow hands, not lumberjacks, and in front leading the pack was Frank Titleman. He and his four *compadres* seemed to be the only ones who were armed, though.

"Maybe they're just coming to watch," Clint said.

"I doubt that," Tom said. "There's gonna be trouble."

When the other competitors saw them, they stopped what they were doing and turned. The judges did the same, and the two male judges suddenly looked worried.

"I hate to say this Clint," Tom said, "but you're the only one on our side who's got a gun."

"I see five guns coming toward us," Clint said. "Nobody else looks armed."

"So five-against-one?" Tom asked. "What the hell kind of odds are those?"

"You're right," Clint said. "I've got them right where I want them."

***

Frank Titleman's frustration from the night before—waiting outside the hotel, then waiting outside the saloon—and never managing to find Clint Adams, had overflowed to this morning, when he proposed something to the Boyce ranch hands.

"Why don't we go and watch some of that lumber-jack competition," he said.

"Why would we wanna do that?" Jensen asked.

"Might be funny watching some of them fall on their asses," Titleman said, "or cut off a finger."

Jensen thought, then said, "You're right, that would be funny."

"See how many of the hands wanna go and have a look," he suggested.

"What about guns?" Jensen asked.

"They won't need guns," Titleman said. "We'll have ours."

Jensen studied Titleman for a minute, then got it.

"Ah, you think Adams is gonna be there."

"I think it's a good bet," Titleman said.

"I'll go and talk to the men."

In the end they managed to get almost twenty of the Boyce ranch hands to go with them to watch the competition. And as they approached the contest site, he was very satisfied to see Clint Adams there.

***

Luke walked over to where Clint and Tom were standing.

"They're lookin' for trouble," he said.

"Think so?" Tom asked.

"Maybe," Clint said, "they're just looking for me."

"You mean because of last night?" Tom asked.

"Last night?"

They explained to him how they'd managed to avoid Titleman and his men the night before, surely frustrating the man.

Luke was holding an axe, and Sally came over holding a saw in both hands.

"Is there gonna be a problem?" she asked.

"Maybe," Clint said. "They might just be coming to watch, but I guess we'll have to wait and see."

TWENTY-NINE

"What's the hold up?" Titleman called out, as they approached. "We came to watch some lumber-jacks."

Marguerite spoke to the cowhands from the judge's stand.

"Are you gentlemen here to observe?" she called out.

The cow men looked up at her, and Titleman stepped forward.

"Are you in charge, ma'am?"

"I'm the head judge," she said.

"Well, me and my friends are here just to watch," he assured her. "We ain't lookin' for no trouble."

"That's fine," she said. "I'll just ask you to remain behind the ropes."

"We can do that, ma'am," Titleman said. "Can't we, boys?"

The cow men nodded their agreement.

"There, see?" Titleman said to her.

"Then I thank you," she said, "and we'll get on with our competition."

"You do that," Titleman said. "After all, that's what we came here to see."

Titleman, his four men, and the hands from the Boyce ranch moved up to the ropes and positioned themselves to watch the proceedings.

"Adams," Titleman greeted. "How's your boy doin'?"

"Your boss send you to see who's winning, Titleman?"

"Mr. Boyce just thinks his boys went to town for some fun," Titleman said. "He don't know we're here watchin'."

Clint looked around at the cow hands, saw a few of them walking away.

"Looks like some of them are going to town," he said. "Losing interest, already."

Titleman looked around and frowned.

"What can I do?" he asked. "I can't make 'em stay and learn somethin' new, can I?"

"That's what you want to do?" Clint asked. "Teach your men something new?"

"Hey," Titleman said, "we can all learn somethin' new, right?"

Jensen and the other three armed men were watching Titleman and Clint with interest. To Clint they looked nervous, which meant they were expecting something to happen.

Tom Allen and Big Luke walked over to a 20 inch in diameter white pine log, with their two man saw, and prepared to start.

Clint was standing with Frank Titleman on his left, but Ted Shelton was once again on his right.

"How long should it take them to saw through that log?" Clint asked.

"Six seconds, maybe less," Ted said.

Clint was shocked.

"That's all?"

"Well," Ted said, "it is only twenty inches around."

Twenty inches sounded pretty big to Clint, but then

he wasn't a lumberjack.

The opposing teams—five of them—took their places at similar logs, and then the starter fired his pistol. In six point two seconds Tom and Luke stepped back, their log cut completely through.

"Wow," Clint said.

"I think we should step away from here," Frank Titleman said.

Clint turned his head and looked at the man.

"What did you have in mind?"

"You were real frustratin' last night," Titleman said. "But today you're not gonna make a fool out of me."

"Why not?" Clint asked. "It was so easy yesterday. What's changed?"

"There's a lot of innocent people around here," Titleman said. "Between you, me and my men, that's a lot of lead that could go flyin' around."

"Not my lead."

"What?"

"My lead only goes where I want it to go," Clint told the man. "You see, Mr. Titleman, I don't miss—ever." That was obviously an exaggeration. There were always unexpected factors that could cause him to miss, but in this case, if he was simply facing five men, he knew he wouldn't miss. He'd just have to be fast enough.

Frank Titleman might be fast with a gun. That only meant that Clint would need to kill him first. The other four would not have Titleman's skill. They would come after. They also wouldn't have their leader's nerve, so even if they got shots off, they'd miss. This was what he'd meant when he said he had them right where he wanted them.

"I'm not going anywhere," Clint said. "If you want to do this here, I'll kill you first, and then your men."

"You have a lot of faith in yourself."

"How do you think I'm still alive after all these years?" Clint

asked.

At that moment both Tom and Luke joined Clint at the ropes. Titleman took a step back. Apparently, something had changed his mind.

"That was impressive," Clint said.

"Yeah," Luke said, "Clyde and his man came in second." He said it with a gleeful grin.

"What's next?" Clint asked.

"Individual choppin'," Tom said.

"So you guys are going to compete against each other?" Clint asked.

"Not exactly," Tom said.

"We'll just both be tryin' to beat Clyde."

"The three of us," Sally said, joining them at that point.

"We just have to make sure that whatever events I don't win," Tom said, "Clyde doesn't win, either."

"Or," Sally added, "like I said before, Clint could just shoot him in the foot—accidentally."

"Clint Adams," Tom Allen said, "never shoots anybody... accidentally."

THIRTY

The single chopping event took longer, because each competitor had to take a turn, and they went two at a time.

Frank Titleman and his men stayed around for most of it, but the cow hands they had brought with them got bored and began to drift away. If Titleman was planning to use them to cause some trouble, it was another plan of his that didn't work. Clint knew that if the man's frustration boiled over, lead was going to fly, regardless of how many innocent bystanders got hit.

During another break Clint saw Marguerite come down from the judges stand, and beckon him over.

"My fellow judges are worried that there might be trouble from those armed cowboys," she said.

"There might have been," Clint said, "but I think I talked them out of it. And it looks like the cow men they brought with them for support have gotten bored and left."

"That's what I told them," she said, "but they wanted me to talk to you because you're the only other man here who is armed."

"I don't think there'll be any trouble here," he said. "At least, not today. Besides, those five men aren't interested in the lumberjacks."

"Oh?"

"It's me they're looking to make trouble for."

"I see."

"That should make you judges feel better."

"Well," she said, "my two colleagues, anyway."

She turned and went back up the steps to the judges stand. Clint went back to his position to watch the chopping event.

Tom, Luke, Sally, and Clyde Norton were all competing. They had to cut through a 12 inch in diameter, 28 foot long aspen log. First one through was the winner.

"How long should this take?" Clint asked Ted.

"Under twenty seconds," Ted said.

Clint asked a question he hadn't thought of, before.

"Who does the timing? The judges?"

"No," Ted said, "there's a fella on the other side of the judges stand with a chronograph. He times the events."

Clint was surprised. He knew that a chronograph was used in the military to measure the speed of artillery. He was surprised that lumberjacks had found another use for it. Then again, he knew of some horse trainers who used them to time their horses.

The chopping took some time, and as Tom, Luke, Sally and Clyde all competed and finished, they had to wait for the remainder of the competitors to also get done.

They joined Clint on the sidelines to wait for the announcement of the winners.

"What do you think?" Clint asked.

"That's easy," Luke said. "Me or Clyde."

"Ha!" Sally said. "I clearly won that event."

Clint looked at Tom, who grinned.

"You?"

"Who else?"

"How about Norton?"

"Clyde was good," Tom said, "but I was better."

"You wanna bet?" Luke asked.

"How much?" Tom asked. "Might as well make some side money."

"Ten dollars," Luke said.

"You got a bet."

"I'll take a piece of that," Sally said.

"Okay," Luke said.

"Clint?"

"Not me," Clint said. "I need to know what I'm doing before I make a bet."

"There's that bitch, Marguerite," Sally said.

"One day," Clint said, "you're going to have to tell me what you have against her."

"Isn't it obvious?" Sally asked. She turned her back to him to look at the judges stand.

"The last event of the day," Marguerite announced, "ended in a tie."

The groans were loud.

"That can't be," Sally said.

"A tie... between who?" Luke yelled out.

"I was getting to that," Marguerite announced.

The other two judges stood up and moved to either side of her.

"The tie is between..." she said, loudly, "Clyde Norton and Tom Allen. We will begin tomorrow's activities with a tie-breaker. That's all for today."

"Damn!" Sally said. "I want to find out what all the times were." She charged the judges stand.

"So do I," Luke said, and followed her.

Clyde came walking over to where Clint and Tom were standing.

"I guess we'll settle this tomorrow mornin'," he said.

"I guess we will."

He slapped Tom on the back and said, "Get a good night's sleep. You're gonna need it."

"You, too."

Clyde walked away.

"What's your relationship with him?" Clint asked.

"I used to work for him," Tom said. "Then I went out on my own and we became competitors."

"And how did he feel about that?"

Tom shrugged. "It was business. I assumed he took it that way."

"Well, it seems like he did," Clint said. "Would he have any reason to kill Ed Fenner?"

"Clyde Norton?" Tom asked. "I can't see why."

"Would Fenner have worked for him, if Clyde got the contract?" Clint asked.

"No," Tom said, without hesitation.

"Why not?"

"Ed would never have worked for Clyde and Clyde wouldn't have hired him. They didn't like each other."

"But he wouldn't have killed him?"

"I said they didn't like each other," Tom said. "You don't kill people just because you don't like them, do you?"

"No, I don't," Clint said, with a shrug, "but maybe that's just me."

THIRTY-ONE

hen they went back to town, Clint waited while Tom, Luke and Sally all had baths. When Sally finished hers, though, she came to Clint's room. As she entered he looked up from the book he was reading, saw that she was wrapped in a towel that barely covered her. She showed shoulder, lots of thigh, and a good portion of the upper slopes of her big breasts.

"You went walking around the hotel like that?" Clint asked.

"Did it raise any eyebrows?"

"Maybe the desk clerk," she said, with a smile. "Nobody else saw me."

"I guess we can be glad for that."

"How about you?" she asked. "Does it raise your eyebrows?"

"A bit."

She unwrapped the towel and dropped it to the floor. Her overripe curves were on display in all their glory, her pale skin still somewhat dappled with bath water, her nipples pink and large.

He put his book down.

"Now my eyebrows are raised."

She approached the bed.

"Hopefully," she said, "that's not all."

He dropped the book to the floor as she crawled onto

the bed with him. As acres of flesh seemed to envelope him, her mouth was avid on his, her hands insistently tearing his shirt off his chest. He ran his hands down his bare back to her butt and squeezed. They rolled around, both involved in getting his boots and trousers off until he was as naked as she was.

Her skin was still damp from her bath, but quickly heated up until there was almost steam coming off of her. Once he was naked she slithered down his body and trapped his hard cock between those big breasts, massaging as she smiled up at him. Then she lowered her head and took him into her mouth, eagerly sucking him wetly.

"Sally," he said, "Sally, Tom and Luke are waiting for us... to..."

She released him from her hot mouth and asked, "To do what?"

"Never mind," he said, putting his hands on her head to guide her back to what she'd been doing, "never mind..."

***

"What took you so long?" Luke demanded, as they came down to the hotel lobby.

"We're starvin'," Tom said.

"So were we," Sally said.

"Were?" Luke asked.

"Are," Clint said. "So <u>are</u> we. Come on. Where are we headed?"

"Where else?" Tom asked. "The Lumberjack's Club."

"Isn't it going to be busy tonight?" Clint asked. "After all, there are a lot of loggers in town."

"It doesn't matter," Tom said. "As one of the founders, I have a regular table."

***

When they got to the Club they did, indeed, find it crowded, but Tom had been right about his table. They were shown to a place that had plenty of room for the four of them, and they all ordered steak dinners.

"Whatever happened to those cowpokes of Boyce's?" Tom asked.

"The hands drifted off when they got bored," Clint said. "The others, Titleman and his men—"

"The ones with the guns?" Sally asked.

Clint nodded.

"They tried to start something, but I talked them out of it."

"You backed them down?" Luke asked. "All five of them?"

"Let's say we probably put the trouble off for another time," Clint said.

"You seem to be doin' that a lot," Tom said. "When's the time gonna come?"

"Probably soon," Clint said. "It seems unavoidable."

"Unless you leave," Sally suggested.

"He can't do that," Luke said.

"Why not?" she asked.

"He's the Gunsmith," Luke said. "He can't run from a fight. If he does and word gets around—"

"—I get it," she said, cutting him off. "There'd be even more men challenging him."

"Exactly," Tom said.

She looked at Clint. Who'd been keeping quiet on the subject.

"That's a terrible way to live," she said.

"I don't have much choice at this point in my life," Clint said. "But I'm not thinking about that, now. I'm still trying to find out who killed Ed Fenner."

"Got anybody in mind?" she asked.

"Well, I did ask Tom about Clyde Norton, earlier today."

"Clyde?" she asked. "Why him?"

"Well, apparently he and Ed Fenner didn't like each other."

"Clyde don't like a lot of people," she said, "and there are probably even more who don't like him. That don't mean he's gonna kill any of 'em."

"You've been around him more than anybody else," Clint said. "Does he have a temper?"

"Sure," she said, "don't most men?"

"A violent temper?" Clint asked. "Ever seen him threaten anybody? Fight with them?"

"You're askin' silly questions, Clint," Sally said. "Lumberjacks are always fightin' with each other. Hell, I've had fights with men I don't like. That don't mean I wanna kill 'em."

Clint looked up, saw Clyde Norton enter the dining room with a few other men.

"Well, he said, "maybe I'll get a chance to ask him myself."

THIRTY-TWO

orton saw Clint and his group, but ignored them. He and his friends were shown to another table.

"Is Clyde one of the founders, also?" Clint asked.

"Oh, yeah," Tom said.

Luke grinned. "We're all founders, Clint."

"I get it."

The waiter came over and set their meals in front of them.

"Finally," Luke said. As the waiter started to walk away Luke grabbed his arm. "Have the cook fire up another steak."

"Yes, sir."

The other three looked at him.

"You haven't even taken a bite of this one," Sally said.

"I know how hungry I am," Luke said.

They all cut into their steaks and started to eat.

**

Halfway through the meal, the waiter came over to the table and said, "Mr. Adams?"

"Yes?"

"Mr. Boyce is out in the hall," the man said. "He's asking to see you."

Clint looked at Tom.

"Does he come here often?" he asked.

"Never," Tom said. "Lumberjacks, remember? Not cattlemen."

"Let me go and see what he wants."

"Want me to come along?" Tom asked.

"No," Clint said, "you eat. I'll be right back."

He got up and followed the waiter out to the hall, where Boyce was waiting. The cattle rancher was wearing trail clothes, rather than an expensive suit. It seemed consistent with the man Clint had talked to out at the ranch.

"Mr. Boyce," Clint said. "What brings you here?"

"Mr. Adams," Boyce said. "I'm probably interrupting your supper. I'm sorry."

"I'd invite you to join me, but—"

"No, no," Boyce said, "I get it. It's Lumberjack's Club, and I'm a cattleman. But maybe we can sit down somewhere?"

Clint looked around, saw a doorway off to one side.

"Let's go in here," he said.

They walked to the door, entered the room, which was empty except for some tables and chairs. Clint thought maybe they used it when the place got really crowded, or perhaps for gaming.

"What's on your mind?" Clint asked.

"Frank Titleman."

"What about him?"

"I fired him and his men today."

"Really. Was that before or after they came out to the competition to try and start trouble?"

"And they took most of my hands with them," Boyce said. "There was no work getting done on my ranch. So when they came back I fired them, told them to get off my land."

"Why tell me?"

"Because Titleman said he was glad I fired him," Boyce said. "It meant he had more time to come after you."

"I see."

"Has he been after you?" Boyce asked.

"Well, let's say he's been... stalking me, the way you stalk an animal you're hunting. He tried to push a fight at the competition, but I wouldn't let him. He was also outside my hotel one night, and the saloon. I avoided him both times."

"I understand," Boyce said. "He's getting frustrated."

"Probably."

"Do you have anyone to back your play?" Boyce asked. "He's got four men."

"Are you offering?"

"Oh, no, not me," Boyce said. "I'm not a gunman. I was just... concerned."

"I'll be fine," Clint said. He didn't tell the rancher that he'd sent a man to Cascade to telegraph for help. "I appreciate the warning."

They stood up and walked out of the room.

"I can't imagine where he and his men could be," Boyce said. "Because of the competition, I imagine the hotel's full."

"They might be camping someplace outside of town," Clint said.

"You know," Boyce said, at the door, "this town needs a lawman. You might consider standing for the job."

"I'm not interested in wearing a badge," Clint said. "Besides, before they hire a lawman they'll have to appoint a town council and elect a Mayor. That'll take a while."

"Well," Boyce said, "it was just a thought. Please, go back to your meal. I hope I haven't ruined it."

"Thanks for the warning," Clint said.,

Boyce left and Clint went back to his table. As he sat, he saw that his plate was gone.

"Where's my supper?" he asked.

"I'm having the waiter bring you a hot one when he brings my second one," Luke said. "That one had gone cold."

"Well... thanks, Luke."

The waiter came over at that moment with two plates, set one down in front Luke and the other in front of Clint.

"Thanks," Clint said, and Luke waved at the waiter. They started to eat again.

"What did Boyce want?" Tom asked, leaning over toward Clint.

"To tell me he fired Frank Titleman and his men."

"When?"

"Today, after they came back from the competition."

"So that means he's gonna have more time to think about killin' you," Tom said.

"Yes."

"I hope Dave Cabrera made it to cascade and sent your telegram."

"So do I," Clint said.

THIRTY-THREE

After supper Tom, Luke and Sally decided to go over to the saloon.

"I'm going to the hotel," Clint said.

"You worried about Titleman?" Tom asked.

"Not worried," Clint said, "but I don't want him and his men walking into the saloon and opening fire. A lot of unarmed innocents could get shot."

"Okay, well, you don't mind if we go, right?" Tom asked. "We need a few drinks after today."

"No, no, you go ahead," Clint said.

Sally kissed him and whispered in his ear, "I'll come to your room after."

"Okay," he said.

The three lumberjacks headed for the saloon, and Clint walked to his hotel.

When he got there, he saw Marguerite Montero walking in just ahead of him. He quickened his step.

"Marguerite," he called, as he entered.

She turned and smiled when she saw him.

"Hello," she said. "I was just coming back from supper."

"So was I. Can I walk you up?"

"Of course."

They went up the stairs and down the hall, past Clint's room to the door of Marguerite's suite.

141

"There you go," he said. "Safe and sound."

"Did you think I was in danger?" She looked amused.

"Well, I didn't know if any of the competitors might want to, you know, have a private word with the judge."

"And do you want to have a private word with the judge?"

"Well..." he said.

"I have a bottle of wine in my suite," she said. "I was going to have a glass before I turn in. But I don't really like to drink alone."

"Is that an invitation?"

"It is."

"Then I accept."

"Good."

She unlocked the door and they went inside.

"Have a seat," she said. "I've got the bottle in the other room, but while I'm there I'm going to change." She stopped at the door and looked at him. "Don't get impatient and leave."

"I won't."

As she went into the other room, Clint walked to the window. Unlike his room, where the window overlooked the alley, her window overlooked the street. The street lamps had been put in front of the hotel were on, and the street looked empty.

He turned and walked to the sofa and chairs, chose one of the armchairs to sit in.

"That's better."

For her judging duties she had been dressed in a shirt, jeans and boots. Now she had changed into a blue dress, very casual, walking in bare feet. She was carrying a bottle of wine and two glasses.

"Now I'm more comfortable," she said, seating herself on the sofa. "I opened this bottle last night. It's very good." She poured two glasses, handed him one.

"Thank you." He sipped it.

"Is it all right?"

"It's fine. It's good."

"Don't tell me," she said, "you're more of a beer man."

"Yes."

"Well," she said, "then more for me. What did you think of today's events?"

"I was very interested."

"Have you ever watched before?"

"No," he said, "this is the first time."

"These men are very good."

"And the woman?"

"Sally?" She shook her head.

"What's wrong with Sally?"

"She's something of a whore," Marguerite said. "If she's a friend of yours, I apologize, but..."

"Don't apologize."

"She's not a friend of yours?"

"I suppose she is," he said. "I've only just met her, but she's friendly with Tom Allen."

"Tom's a good man," she said. "He should have better taste."

He decided to change the subject.

"So, as a head judge are you allowed to have any opinions?" he asked.

"Not really," she said. "At least, not about anyone who's involved. But you're not involved, are you?"

"Nope," he said. "Just a spectator."

She sipped her wine.

"So what do you think?" he pushed.

"Tom's good," she said. "So's Clyde Norton. I expect one of them to win."

"Not Big Luke?"

"Luke's a good man, a good worker," she said. "Dependable. But he's not fast enough in any of these events to be a winner."

"Anybody else?"

"No," she said. "The others are trying, but they're not in the same class as Tom and Clyde."

"So Tom or Clyde will get the job," Clint said, "the Boyce contract."

"And then lots of other men will get jobs, too," he said.

"Yes," she said, "and a lot of the same men."

"Would Clyde hire Luke?"

"Probably. Like I said, he's a good worker. He wouldn't hire Sally, though."

"So I've heard."

"How is your investigation, going?" she asked. "Are you close to finding out who killed Mr. Fenner?"

"Not yet," Clint said. "You don't have any information, do you? Anything you might have remembered?"

"Sorry, no," she said.

"What about Clyde Norton?"

"What about him?"

"Think he could be a killer?"

"If he got mad enough," she said. "Sure. If he had something against Ed. But before you ask, I don't know that he did."

Clint finished his wine and set the glass down.

"More?" she asked.

"I wouldn't want you to waste it." He stood up. "I better be going."

"Why?" she asked. "Is someone waiting for you?"

"No," he said. "Just a book."

"What book?"

"Robert Louis Stevenson short stories."

"Oh? I'm impressed. A legend of the old west who reads literature."

"You've read Stevenson?"

"I have."

"I'm impressed," he said. "A lumberjack competition judge who reads literature."

She blushed and said, "I guess I deserved that."

She stood up with him and walked him to the door, but she didn't open it.

"You need rest, too," he said.

"I can rest," she said, "later."

"Later?"

She nodded.

"After," she said.

"After what?"

She put her hand on his left hand, then ran it up his arm to his shoulder, until finally she pressed it against his cheek, softly, tenderly.

"After," she whispered, then leaned in to kiss him.

It was gentle at first, then she kissed him on the corners of the mouth before kissing his mouth again, this time with more pressure, more insistence that he was not able to resist.

He put his arms around her and kissed her back, holding her tightly, her breasts crushed against his chest. Her kiss became fierce, and he matched it with ferocity of his own. He could feel her nails digging into him, right through his shirt.

She pushed away from him, then took his hand and led him to the doorway of the bedroom.

"Neither one of us is going to get much rest, are we?" he asked her.

"Sure we are," she assured him, "after."

145

THIRTY-FOUR

In the bedroom was a giant, comfortable looking bed, with the bedpost Clint always needed to hang his holster on.

"Does your gun always need to be within arm's reach?" she asked.

"Yes," he said, "always."

"Even in bed?"

"Especially in bed."

"Well," she said, "I don't think you'll be needing it tonight."

She reached behind her, undid her dress and let it fall to the floor. Obviously, when she had gone into the room earlier to get the wine and change her clothes, she had also left her underwear behind. She stood before him, tall, leggy, naked, with breasts he might not have thought would be as big as they were—not melons, but nice round, ripe peaches. Her nipples were dark brown, but what caught his eye even more was the black tangle of hair between her thighs. She stood there for a few moments, letting him have a good, long look.

"As a head judge," she said, then, "I'm judging that you seem to be a bit overdressed."

"I think you're right."

He started to unbutton his shirt but she said, "Sit, I'll help you with your boots."

He sat at the foot of the bed, and she slid his boots and socks off, but she didn't stop there. She unbuttoned his shirt, slid her hands inside it so she could slide it off his shoulders. She rubbed her palms over his chest, then moved her hands down to his waist to undo his belt and buttons. She slid his trousers down and discarded them, then rubbed her hands over his bare thighs. Using her nails, she traced the outline of his hard cock inside his underwear, then pulled the top of the garment down so that he popped out.

"Oh yes," she said, taking it in her hand and stroking it lightly. "Let's get these off, by all means."

He lifted his hips so she could slide his underwear off, and then he was as naked as she was.

Again she ran her palms over him, his chest, his belly, his thighs, before once again taking hold of his now fully hard cock.

"You're a beautiful man," she said.

"And you're a beautiful woman."

She stretched up to kiss him, all the while maintaining her hold on his penis, continuing to stroke it. He put his hands on her, feeling the smoothness of her skin, ran them up and down her back. Then, as the kiss and the stroking went on, he slid a hand between them, down between her thighs, where he found her hot and wet. He stroked her, then slid one finger inside of her so that she gasped, and tensed. She shuddered, and became even more wet, drenching his hand.

She broke the kiss and released her hold on his cock, but only so she could rise up, slide into his lap, and engulf him in her hungry pussy. She sat down on him hard, taking him completely inside with a loud, guttural groan that matched his own.

He slid his hands beneath her to palm her butt cheeks,

which had become slick with her wetness as she rode him, bouncing up and down on his lap.

"Oh, God," she groaned, "I needed this..." She leaned into him, pressed her mouth to his ear. "I meant for this to be more... romantic... but really I just want to... fuck..."

"Well, if I'm any judge," he replied, "you're very good at it."

***

"Oh," Marguerite said, later, "oh, oh, oh..."

They were lying side-by-side on their backs in the big bed, and she was stroking his left thigh with her right hand.

"I feel so much better."

"I'm glad," he said.

"And it's all because of you," she went on. "I've needed this for a long time."

"Don't you know any other men?"

"I know a lot of men," she said, "but none who I want to do this with. But when we met... well, I just knew..."

She patted his thigh, then pulled her hand away.

"I'd like to go to sleep now," she said.

"That's fine," he said, "I could use some—"

"No, I mean you should go."

He turned his head and looked at her. "We're done?"

"Yes."

He sat up, looked down at her.

"It's a big comfortable bed."

"Clint," she said, "you probably have Sally waiting for you in your room."

"Sally's in the saloon with Tom and Luke."

"But she'll be back," she said. "You should be there waiting for her." Then she smiled. "And smelling of me."

When Clint got back to his room he sat on his bed and realized he did smell like Marguerite. He wondered if he should go downstairs and have a bath before Sally got back?

He took off his shirt and put it in his saddlebag, then took out a fresh one and put it on. That might help. Of course, if Sally did come to his room, and wanted sex, and they got naked, would she smell Marguerite on his skin? Maybe the desk clerk had some lilac water or something that he could splash on himself—

There was a knock on his door, then, and he realized it was too late. That had to be Sally.

Of course, just in case it wasn't, he took his gun to the door with him.

"Who is it?"

"Sally," she whispered, but loudly. "Lemme in!"

He unlocked the door, opened it a crack, saw her in the hall alone, and then opened it all the way.

"Sally—"

"I am beat!" she said. She started to remove her clothes as soon as she entered the room and then, completely naked, she crawled onto the bed and promptly fell asleep.

Clint realized she was not only exhausted, but drunk as well. As he closed the door and slid his gun back into his holster, she started to snore.

There was not going to be a problem tonight. Maybe in the morning, but apparently, not tonight.

THIRTY-FIVE

Clint slept remarkably well that night, and woke with Sally's leg over his. He lifted his arm to his nose and sniffed himself. He still smelled like Marguerite. Since there was only one thing he could think of to rub all over himself to hide the smell, he rolled Sally onto her belly, and then crawled atop her. He rubbed his body on her until his cock got hard, and then began to run that along the cleft between her meaty buttocks. She moaned and began to wriggle her bottom against him.

He slid his cock between her thighs, kissed the back of her neck, and shoulders while fucking her that way. And then she lifted her hips off the bed, which he took as an invitation. He slid his penis further up between her thighs until he was poking at her vagina, which was already wet. Deftly, he allowed the spongy head of his cock to slide in and, as she moaned and spread her arms out, glided into her wet pussy the rest of the way. With her face in her pillow, all she could smell were the sheets.

She turned her head to the side so she could say, "Mmm, this is quite a way to wake up."

"You just relax," he told her, "and let me do all the work."

"Mmm," she moaned, "I can do that, all right..."

He began to slide in and out of her, slowly at first, and then as he moved faster and faster she got onto her

151

knees and elbows. This gave him better purchase, and also allowed her to rock back against him every time he drove into her.

He hoped that by the time he was done he would smell completely of Sally, and not of Marguerite, at all.

***

Sally's orgasms were wet and aromatic, which Clint considered good. Any hint of Marguerite that might have been in the air was gone by the time they were done.

"Oh God!" Sally said, rolling onto her back on the dry side of the bed. "You really wanted that."

"I did," he said. "I really did."

She opened her arms to him and gathered him into her breasts for a deep, long kiss.

"I need a bath," she said, "even though I'm gonna be rolling and cuttin' logs today."

"Yes, I need one, too."

"Can you go down and make the arrangements?" she asked. "And then you can have breakfast and I'll get over to the field—unless you rather I eat with you than with them?"

"No, no," he said, "you go and eat with your... competitors? Partners?"

"Some of each," she said. "Whew. Don't know how you can stand the way I smell."

"You smell like a woman," he told her. "There's nothing wrong with that."

"You're a real man, Clint Adams!"

He got dressed, wearing the same clothes he'd put on after his bath. He didn't want to have to come back to the room, he wanted to go right to breakfast.

***

They had their baths in separate tubs, even though his cock got hard as she got out of hers all pink and clean.

"Look at you," she said, "ready, again."

"Well," he said, "I'm looking at you."

She knelt by his tub, took hold of his cock and leaned into kiss him, holding it tight. She stroked it and said, "I wish I had the time to give this a proper goin' over, Mr. Adams, but you'll have to wait until tonight."

"I'll do my best," he said, stroking one of her naked breasts, pinching the pink nipple.

"Hey, stop that!" She got back to her feet and quickly got dressed. "I'll see you out there."

After she left, he settled into his tub and waited for his erection to wilt, then got out and dressed. He couldn't believe it, but he'd managed to have sex with both women, and not get into trouble.

It was obvious that Marguerite had simply used him to scratch an itch, and at the same time had tried to get Sally's goat. He was going to have to be careful of that woman.

He dried off, dressed, and went to breakfast.

THIRTY-SIX

He went to the café and ate breakfast alone. Over steak-and-eggs, he hoped that Dave Cabrebra would be getting back from Cascade with the answer to his telegram sometime that day. He'd love to know that Talbot Roper was at least on the way. So far he considered himself a complete failure as a private detective as he was no closer to finding out who killed Ed Fenner.

After breakfast he went outside and looked up and down the empty street. This town was still a long way from becoming a going concern, and he wondered if it was ever going to make it, at all.

At that moment he saw a buckboard carrying the two male judges come down the street and stop in front of the hotel. Moments later Marguerite came out. The taller of the two judges got down, helped her up, then climbed up and sat next to her. The shorter judge snapped the reins, and they drove the buckboard out of town. He had the feeling Marguerite knew he was watching, yet she never looked over at him. He had an idea why she had been named the head judge. She was cold.

He looked across the street, saw the undertaker's door open and the man step out. Abruptly, Clint trotted across the street to catch him before he went anywhere.

"Mr. Winston."

The man turned, frowned, then brightened.

"Mr. Adams. What can I do for you?"

"I was wondering if anybody had come to your place to look at the body of Ed Fenner?"

"A few of his friends."

"Do you know their names?"

"No, sorry," Winston said. "I'm afraid all these lumberjacks look alike to me."

"Did anybody say anything, uh, suspicious?" Clint asked.

"Like what?"

"Like maybe they were glad he was dead?"

"No," Winston said, "all the men who came to see Mr. Fenner seemed pretty sad."

"And when they looked at the body, were you with them?"

Winston hesitated, then said, "Most of them."

"What's that mean?"

"There was one man who wanted to view the body, but just when he asked another person came in and... distracted me."

"Another person?"

Winston looked embarrassed.

"A woman."

"Okay," Clint said, "this is very important, Mr. Winston. What did the woman look like?"

"I can do better than that," the undertaker said, "I can tell you her name."

"You knew her?"

Winston nodded.

"Most people do."

***

Clint went to the livery, saddled Eclipse and rode out

to where the events were being held. It was only a short distance, but he didn't feel like walking. And the ride would give Eclipse a little bit of exercise.

Once he left Eclipse with the other horses, he walked to the field to watch the first event—the tie breaker between Tom Allen and Clyde Norton.

"Thought you were gonna miss your friend's event," Ted Shelton said.

"I wouldn't miss this," Clint said, "not after watching all day yesterday."

"Say Ted," Clint said, "did you know Ed Fenner?"

"Fenner, yeah," Ted said, "I knew him. I heard about what happened. Terrible thing. Oh, I get it. You're the one tryin' to find out who did it."

"That's right."

"Well, ask me whatever you want," Ted said. "I sure wanna try to help."

"Do you know anybody who would have hated Ed enough to kill him with an axe?"

"I don't know anyone who hated him, period."

"Are you acquainted with most of these people?"

"Sure," Ted said. "We know each other."

"And the judges?"

"Well, yeah," Ted said, "they've been around. I don't know them well, but I know who they are."

"Tell me about Clyde."

"Clyde Norton knows what he wants, and he ain't afraid to go after it," Ted said.

"And would he kill for what he wants?"

Ted looked Clint in the eye and asked, "What man wouldn't kill for what he really wants?"

"Well, some won't," Clint said.

"If a man won't," Ted said, "then he ain't much of a man. But hey, that's just my opinion."

"That's what I asked you for, Ted," Clint said. "Thanks for your help."

"Sure."

As Tom Allen and Clyde Norton positioned themselves to compete to break their tie, both Luke and Sally came over to where Clint was standing.

"You mind if we watch with you?" Sally asked.

"Hey, the more support we can give him," Clint said, "the better, right?"

"Tom needs to beat Clyde right here," Luke said. "I think it'll really hurt Clyde to lose this."

"Couldn't happen to a nicer guy, as far as I'm concerned," Sally said.

THIRTY-SIX

The starter fired his pistol and Tom and Clyde began chopping furiously. But Clint saw something in Clyde's demeanor that he didn't see in Tom's. Clyde kept looking over to see how far along Tom was. Meanwhile, Tom just kept his head down and went chop-chop-chop until he was done.

To the naked eye it looked like another tie when it was over.

"Whoo!" Luke said. "I dunno!"

"Tom got it!" Sally said.

"You think so?" Clint asked.

"I know so," Sally said. "Clyde was nervous. He kept looking at Tom."

"I noticed that," Clint said.

"The judges have their heads together," Ted said.

Tom and Clyde shook hands at the end, then went to stand before the judge's stand.

"This is tight, again," Luke said.

Sally gripped Clint's left arm, digging her nails in.

"It's gotta be Tom," she said.

He slid his left arm around her waist, mainly to get her to stop using her nails on him.

"Here they come," Luke said, as the judges broke and Marguerite stepped forward.

"The winner of this tie breaker is... Clyde Norton!"

"No!" Sally yelled.

Tom looked over at her and shrugged.

"Damn!" Luke said.

All the lumberjacks moved forward, to get ready for the next event.

"Come on," Luke said to Sally, "we gotta go."

"Good luck," Clint said, as they moved away.

"That was rough," Ted said. "The judges really argued over that one."

"Did they?" Clint asked. "I was watching Tom and Clyde."

"Marguerite was really arguin' her point," Ted said.

Clint wished he had been watching. Had she argued for Tom and lost, or argued for Clyde and won?

***

There were a couple of more events on the field, one of which was won by Tom, and the other by Luke. After that, it was time to move down to the river.

As everyone started walking that way, Clint found himself walking next to Tom.

"I haven't seen Dave Cabrera yet today," he said. "I thought he'd be back by now."

"He'll be back," Tom assured him, "as long as nobody got in his way."

"That's what I'm wondering about."

"Dave will be here," Tom said. "He's a good rider, and he's reliable."

"I hope you're right."

"Have you found out anythin' else that might help you figure out who killed Ed?"

"I keep talking to people. I've got a couple of ideas," Clint admitted, "but I can't deny I'd feel better getting some professional help."

"From your friend Roper?"

Clint nodded.

"Well, I hope you get it," Tom said, "but right now I need some help of my own."

"What kind?"

"I need Clyde Norton to fall into the river!"

"How close is it?" Clint asked.

"I think we're neck-and-neck," Tom said. "Luke winnin' that one event helped, I think."

"Well," Clint said, "it's like Sally keeps sayin', I could accidentally shoot Clyde in the foot."

"Let's keep that aside for later," Tom said, "if I can't get this done on my own. It might come to that as a last resort."

"I was kidding," Clint said.

Tom looked at him. "I'm not," he said. Then ran on ahead to the river."

THIRTY-SEVEN

The Rogue River was filled with floating logs. On the shore were the men—and the woman—who were going to walk on them. Or were they going to run? Clint wasn't sure.

But Clint wasn't thinking about the events that would take place on the river. He was thinking about the three judges, standing up on a hill from where they would observe. And he was thinking about David Cabrera, where and how he was. Did he get to Cascade? Did he send the telegram to Talbot Roper? Or had something befallen him, either on the way there or on the way back?

Spectators had to take up positions where they could watch. They weren't permitted to go right down by the river's edge. And while it occurred to Clint that was where the judges probably should be for the best vantage point, the three of them remained at the top of a hill.

Clint found himself a flat spot that was actually halfway up—or down—a hill, and he stood alone to watch. He sort of wished he had taken Ted along with him, for more commentary. As it stood now, he wasn't quite sure what the events would entail, except that he saw some men—Tom Allen included—who were walking on logs, bouncing on them, as if testing them out for balance, or simply practicing for the upcoming events.

In point of fact, Clint wasn't actually sure he absolutely needed Talbot Roper. After talking with the undertaker, he thought he had a good idea who was behind the murder of Ed Fenner, if not who had actually wielded the axe.

Something was holding up the action, and some of the lumberjacks came back on shore and began milling around, looking up at the judges, and shrugging their shoulders.

Clint decided the best thing for him to do was go back to town, ask some more questions, and maybe even be there where Dave Cabrera finally got back. From the looks of things the contest was not going to start any time soon, and he might be able to return before it was all over.

He turned and started up the hill.

***

Clint rode back into town, which was even emptier than usual, with most people out by the river to watch the events. He rode to the livery and took care of Eclipse before returning to his hotel.

"Anybody looking for me?" he asked the desk clerk, who seemed surprised to see him.

"Uh, no, sir. No one has asked."

"Okay, thanks."

"Uh, will you be in your room if anyone does ask?"

"Just for a little while."

But when he went to the second floor he didn't let himself into his own room. He walked to the end of the hall and easily forced the door of Marguerite's room, slipping inside and closing the door behind him.

He did a quick search of the suite, checking drawers of the chest in the bedroom, looking underneath all of

Marguerite's filmy underthings. He found nothing more incriminating than underwear with hearts on them.

Coming back into the main room of the suite, he sat down in an armchair and relaxed. As long as Marguerite was the head judge out at the competition, there was no danger of her walking in on him. He didn't know what he had expected to find, he'd just thought to take advantage of the town being virtually empty and have a look around.

Finally, he left Marguerite's suite and headed back down the hall. Briefly, he thought about breaking into Tom's room, or Luke's room, but if he didn't trust them, then he couldn't trust anybody. And Sally didn't have her own room, so she had no place to hide anything.

He gave the desk clerk a slight wave on his way through the lobby, stopped just outside the hotel. He was hoping to see Dave Cabrera riding into town, but it wasn't to be. The street was empty as ever.

Stepping off the boardwalk into the street, he headed for the lumberjack hotel, but took a slight detour to stop in the alley where Ed Fenner's body had been found. There was still plenty of blood soaked into the dirt there, and he could see some axe cuts in the wall of the saloon, indicating that at least a couple of wild swings had missed before finally connecting. He studied the cuts in the wall. They were deep, and thick. It was a large axe that was used, and a heavy one.

Clint left the alley and went over to the saloon. Above the door was a sign that said BLACKIE'S SALOON. Blackie was there behind the bar, all alone as there were no lumberjacks in the place, not while the competition going on.

"Don't tell me it's all over," Blackie said, hopefully.

"Nope."

The man's shoulders slumped.

"But you can give me a beer," Clint said. "I just got tired of watching, and waiting."

"Comin' up."

Blackie drew the cold beer and set it on the bar.

"Can't wait til that nonsense out there is over and I get some customers back," he said.

"What about once the job on the Boyce ranch starts?" Clint asked. "Won't that cut into your business?"

"Nah," the bartender said, "after a day's work them guys'll be cravin' a beer. I'll be busy most nights." He smiled. "That cow puncher saloon across the street won't, though. Haw!"

Clint drank some beer, then leaned his elbows on the bar.

"Blackie, have you had any thoughts, maybe any memories of anybody arguing with Ed Fenner the night he was killed?"

Blackie took the same posture and said, "Naw, I ain't been able ta think of nobody. Ed was a good ol' boy, and a hard worker. Don't know why anybody would wanna kill him."

"Yeah, that's what I thought," Clint said. "Doesn't seem to be any reason for anybody to kill him." He drank some more beer. "But somebody did."

THIRTY-EIGHT

lint took his time finishing his beer, figuring he'd head back out to the river once his glass was empty.

"Blackie, you ever see Fenner with a woman?"

"What, Ed? With a gal? Naw, never. Why, somebody tell you he had a gal?"

"Well," Clint said, "the undertaker said a woman went over there to look at the body."

"That a fact?" Blackie asked. "Who was it?"

"He didn't say," Clint said. Well, it wasn't really a lie. The undertaker didn't know the woman's name, he had simply described her to Clint.

"Huh, that's funny," Blackie said. "Why would a woman wanna see his body?"

"That's what I was wondering."

"Well, maybe you can find her and ask."

"Maybe," Clint said. He finished his beer and pushed the mug away. "I better head back out. I don't want Tom to think I wasn't supporting him."

As he left the saloon he saw a group of riders coming up the street. He stopped to watch, saw that it was Frank Titleman and his men, but there were six riders. Usually, with Titleman, there were five. He watched them come toward him, and thought he recognized the sixth man.

It was Dave Cabrera, and he was in a bad way. As they got closer, Clint could see he was battered and bruised, and barely conscious.

The riders reined in their horses in front of him.

"Adams," Titleman said, "just the man I was lookin' for."

"You've gone too far this time, Titleman," Clint said.

"Wha—oh, you mean this fella here?" Titleman asked, indicating the half-conscious Cabrera. "We ran into him outside of town and he told us he was a friend of yours. So we made him feel welcome. Didn't we boys?"

"We sure did," Jensen said.

The other three nodded, and one of them put a hand on Cabrera's shoulder to keep him from falling off his horse.

"That's okay, Lenny," Titleman said, "you can let him go, now."

The man removed his hand and Cabrera promptly fell off his horse before Clint could do a thing to catch him.

"You wanna come and get him?" Titleman asked. He and his partners were surrounding the fallen man with their horses. Clint would have had to bull his way through them.

"Come on," Titleman said, "come and pick him up."

"What do you want, Titleman?" Clint asked.

"I want you to stop runnin', Adams," Titleman said. "Just stand there."

"And let you shoot me down?"

"Well," Titleman said, "not let us, but that's how it would end up."

"You think so," Clint said, "but before we get to that I need to ask you if you had anything to do with killing Ed Fenner."

"Ed who?" Titleman asked. "Oh, you mean the lumberjack who got chopped up? I didn't even know him,

Adams. Why would I kill him? And if I did kill him, he'd be full of lead. I wouldn't use an axe."

"And that goes for the rest of your boys?"

The other men nodded and Jensen said, "We didn't know the guy. Why would we wanna know a lumberjack?"

"Okay," Clint said, "so now you boys have a choice. Turn around and ride out so I take care of my friend, or join him on the ground when I shoot you out of your saddles."

Titleman laughed, while the other four men did not look so amused.

"Come on, Adams," he said, "you're still tryin' to run away. We're gonna dismount and face you right here in the street, and then we'll even get your friend some help when it's all over. How's that?"

"Not good enough," Clint said. "There are five of you, and only one of me. I get to choose the parameters, not you."

"The para-what?" Jensen asked.

"I say where we stand and how we do this," Clint said, making it clearer.

"So say it," Titleman said. "I'm gettin' real tired of chasin' you and waitin' for you."

"Well, where we do it is right here," Clint said, "and the time is right now."

"Wha—" Titleman started, but there was no more time for him to speak.

Clint drew and started to fire, quickly, efficiently. There were five men, his gun had six bullets, and he didn't want to empty his gun, so he fired five times.

His first bullet took Titleman high in the chest, but off to the left because just at that moment the man's horse shied, saving his life. But the impact of the bullet still knocked him from the saddle, and when he landed, the wind was knocked out of him.

In quick succession the other bullets each hit one man. Clint did not miss once. Jensen went over backwards and was dead before he hit the ground. The other three men all took bullets square in the chest, fell from their horses, and were dead before they hit the ground.

The horses all shied and whinnied; two of them reared up, one of them came down with its front hooves just missing Dave Cabrera's head. The other horse caved in a dead man's skull. After that, the six horses split and ran off in all directions, leaving six men lying in the street, only two of them alive.

Dave Cabrera rolled over and moaned.

Frank Titleman was suddenly able to take a breath, and when he did he rolled to his left so he could reach for the gun on his right hip.

"Don't!" Clint shouted, but Titleman didn't listen.

This was exactly the reason Clint had not fired all six shots. If his gun had been empty at this moment, Titleman would have killed him.

But he fired for a sixth time, and killed Frank Titleman, instead.

THIRTY-NINE

Blackie came running out of the saloon.

"What the hell—"

Clint bent over Dave Cabrera, who looked up at him with pained eyes.

"Take it easy," Clint said. "You'll be fine."

"Jesus—" Cabrera said.

Clint stood and ejected the empty shells from his gun, reloaded and holstered it. Only then did he turn to Blackie.

"No doctor in this town, right?"

"That's right," Blackie said, "but the undertaker, Millard, has done some doctorin'. Is he shot?"

Clint checked Cabrera over.

"I ain't shot," the man said. "Just beat up, some."

"Beat up a lot, I'd say," Clint said. "Blackie, can you help me get him to the undertaker?"

"Sure thing," Blackie said, stepping into the street.

Together they lifted the injured man and half carried, half dragged him across to the undertaker's office. Clint knocked on the door and Millard Winston answered.

"Bring him inside," the undertaker said, without asking any questions.

They dragged him inside and Winston cleared room for them to sit him down next to a table.

"What happened?" the undertaker asked.

"He got beat up," Clint said, "and then fell off a horse."

"Looks like he fell off a horse a few times, and then got dragged," Winston said. "I'll see what I can do to patch him up."

"I need to talk to him," Clint said.

"That'll have to wait."

"Just one que—"

"Here now!" the undertaker snapped, and caught Cabrera as he fell over. "Help me get him on the table."

The three of them lifted Cabrera and laid him on the table on his back.

"He's out now," Millard Winston said, "so you're gonna have to wait."

"Yeah, okay," Clint said. "I'll be back."

"Good," Winston said, "because I ain't got room for him, here. Once I patch him up you'll have to take him."

"I'll take care of him," Clint said, "get him into the hotel."

"Okay," Winston said, "better gimme about a half an hour."

"Come on back to the saloon," Blackie said, "I'll give you a beer."

"We've got five dead men in the street," Clint said. "How do we get rid of them?"

"I'll have it taken care of," The undertaker said. Then he looked at Clint. "You killed them? Was that the shootin' I heard?"

"Yes," Clint said, "they didn't leave me much of a choice."

"You ain't gotta explain it to me," Winston said. "I ain't the law. I'll see you in about an hour."

"Thanks, Millard," Blackie said.

He and Clint left the undertaker's office and headed

back across to the saloon, skirting the dead bodies along the way.

***

Clint drank another beer at the bar with Blackie, who at one point walked to the front window of the saloon and looked out.

"What's going on?" Clint asked.

"Coupla guys takin' the bodies away," Blackie said.

"You know them?"

"I recognize them," the bartender said, coming back to the bar. "They work for Millard."

"There's people in town who aren't lumberjacks or cowboys?" Clint asked. "Who don't work in the saloons, or the Lumberjack Club?"

"These fellas do odd jobs," Blackie said. "That's why Millard uses them." Back behind the bar he asked, "You want another one?"

"No, I've got to get across the street and take Cabrera off the undertaker's hands."

"Did you find out if he did what you wanted him to do?" the bartender asked.

"No, that's what I have to ask him, once he can talk," Clint said. He finished his beer and shoved the empty mug across the bar to Blackie.

He headed for the batwing doors.

"It ain't been an hour, yet!" Blackie called after him.

"That's okay," Clint said, waving an arm. "It's close enough."

FORTY

When Clint got back to the undertaker's, David Cabrera was sitting up in a chair, conscious. He had some bandages on his face and, Clint was sure, underneath his shirt.

"How's he doing?" he asked the undertaker.

"I think he's got a couple of broken ribs," Winston said. "Not much that can be done about that. I wrapped him up tight to try to give him some relief. Cuts and bruises on his face. I took care of those. He'll live."

Clint approached Cabrera.

"How are you feeling?"

"Rotten." He touched his face gingerly.

"I'm sorry about this," Clint said.

"It wasn't your fault."

"We can probably argue that point," Clint said. "Have you got a place to stay?"

"No," Cabrera said, "I gave up my room when I rode out."

"Well, come back to the hotel with me. If we can't get you a room, I'll give you mine."

"I ain't gonna argue," Cabrera said. "I gotta lie down. The ride was bad enough, but this..."

"I understand." Clint looked at the undertaker. "What do I owe you, Millard?"

"Nothin'," Winston said, "but if he dies, I get the business."

"Deal."

"That goes for you, too."

"Understood." He turned his attention to Cabrera. "Come on, I'll help you walk."

With his left arm around the man's waist—so that his gunhand was free—he helped Cabrera across the street to the hotel and sat him down in the lobby before approaching the desk clerk.

"You got any rooms?" he asked.

"Gee, I'm sorry, no, Mr. Adams," the clerk said. "With the lumberjack thing goin' on—"

"Never mind," Clint said. "I'll take him up to my room."

"Yessir."

He got Cabrera out of the chair, helped him up the stairs and down the hall. Once in the room, he deposited him on the bed and helped him take his boots off.

"You go ahead and get some rest," Clint said, "but before you do, can you tell me if you got that telegram sent?"

"I did," Cabrera said, with his eyes closed.

"And did you get an answer?"

"Yeah," Cabrera said, "from some woman who said that your friend was out of town, but she'd leave him a message."

That didn't help much, but he wasn't about to shoot the messenger. It wasn't Cabrera's fault, and he'd taken a beating for his trouble.

"Okay, relax, then," Clint said. "I'll bring you something to eat when I come back."

There was no answer. Cabrera was already asleep.

Clint returned to the Rogue River. He couldn't get back to his previous vantage point, so he just watched from the top of the hill as some men seemed to be running on the logs, keeping them rolling beneath them. He wasn't sure what the object of the contest was supposed to be, but one-by-one the men were falling into the river, so he assumed the last one standing would be a winner.

Abruptly, as he was watching, Sally came up alongside him; she was dripping wet.

"Don't say it," she warned him.

Her shirt was sticking to her, so that he large breasts were distinctly outlined underneath. He could even see her large nipples poking at the shirt. Her hair was wet and hanging down past her shoulders, reminding him of how she had looked in the bath.

"You look great."

"That all you can say?"

"How'd you do?"

"I'm wet, so I lost."

"Tom and Luke?"

"Luke's a bull," she said, "he tried it, but he fell right away."

"And Tom?"

She pointed to the river.

"There's three of 'em left down there," she said. "He's the one on the right."

Once she said that, Clint was able to recognize his friend.

"Neither of the other two look like Norton," he said.

"Clyde's like Luke," she said, "too big to keep his balance. He fell early."

"That's good," Clint said. "How many events left

after this?"

"Only one," she said.

"What is it?"

"Logrolling."

"And what's that?"

"Two men on one log, trying to knock each other off."

"Can they use their hands?"

"No. They have to use their feet, trying to spin the log and throw the other man off balance."

"Sounds interesting."

"Yeah," Sally said, "if Tom takes that event, he should win the whole competition."

"Is Norton in that event?"

"He is, but he's not good on the logs," she said. "The way I figure it, the only way he can win the whole thing is for Tom to lose that last event."

"Do we know who Tom will be going against?"

"Not yet," she said. "We've still gotta wait for this one to be done."

And as she said that they looked down at the river. One of the other men had already fallen. Now there was only Tom and another man, and fairly soon the other man fell.

Tom Allen was the winner.

Sally turned and hugged Clint, crushing her breasts to his chest so hard he could feel her nipples. He hugged her back.

"He won! He won!" she said.

"Should we go down?"

"No," she said, "if we're not competing we shouldn't go down to the river's edge."

"Aren't you in the logrolling?"

"Not me," she said. "I just tried this event for fun,

178

but with somebody else on the log?" She shook her head. "I'd be in the water before I knew it."

They looked around and saw that other spectators were also waving their arms in approval of Tom's victory.

"Where'd you go?" she asked. "We noticed you were gone for a while."

"I went to town to see if Dave Cabrera had come back."

"And did he?"

"He did," he said, "but it didn't turn out the way I wanted it to."

"So your detective friend ain't comin'?"

"No." he decided not to tell her about the beating Cabrera had taken, and about the shooting. Leave that for later.

"It don't matter," she said. "You're gonna find the killer."

"I hope you're right."

FORTY-ONE

"**S**ally," Clint said, while they waited for the logrolling to begin, "tell me more about Clyde Norton."

"Whataya wanna know?"

"Was he ever married?"

"Clyde? No."

"How long were you with him?"

"Coupla months," she said. "Took me that long to find out what he was really like."

"And what was that?"

"Not the kinda man I wanted to be around," she said. "There was the right way, the wrong way, and then there was Clyde's way—and I didn't like that."

"Do you know what woman he was with before you?"

"Some floozy," she said. "I didn't ask."

"What about after you."

"You really wanna know?"

"That's why I'm asking."

"After me came the head judge, Marguerite."

"Really?" Clint asked. He looked over to where the judges were standing. "Is that legal? I mean, should she be judging at all, let alone being the head judge?"

"Well," Sally said, "supposedly they ain't together anymore."

"Is that why you don't like each other?" he asked.

"Because you were with the same man?"

"There's other reasons," she said. "She probably already told you what she thinks of me. Well, she's a stuck-up bitch who thinks she's better than everybody else. And she's cold, like ice."

Clint knew that much about Marguerite.

"Hey," Sally said, "they're gonna start."

"How many are competing?"

"It's the last event, and only the ones who have a chance to win the whole thing are in it."

Clint looked down the hill, saw four men standing on the river's edge. One was Tom, and one looked like Clyde."

"Who are the other two?"

"Del Shearen and Happy Axler. Technically, they have a chance, but really, they don't. It's only Clyde and Tom."

Clint watched the way they lined up.

"Tom's not going to be on a log with Clyde."

"No," she said. "He drew Del."

"Can Clyde beat Happy?"

"Actually," Sally said, "he might be able to."

"How?" Clint asked. "You said he's a bull, with bad balance."

She looked at Clint, brushed her wet hair out of her eyes.

"He has a chance to scare him off the log."

"Well, if he does, he'll have to go against Tom, right?" Clint said. "I mean, if Tom wins."

"Tom will win," she said. "Just watch."

***

The sun was bright. While the event went on, Sally's clothes and hair were drying out.

Clint watched, fascinated that two men could run that way on a log, rolling it, spinning it, keeping their balance, trying to knock each other off. He didn't think he'd ever be able to do that.

"There he goes," she said.

"Who?"

"Happy," she said. "Clyde's got 'im."

Just as she said it, Happy Axler went flying off his log, into the water. A split second later, Clyde also went into the water.

"Clyde fell!" Clint said.

"It don't matter," she said. "Happy fell first. Clyde wins. Now it's up to Tom."

Tom Allen and Del Shearen were working their log like two madmen. At one point Tom waved his arms and looked like he was going off, but he regained his balance, seemed to redouble his efforts, and in moments Del Shearen was in the water. Tom threw his arms in the air. Onlookers cheered, many of them as if they knew they were now going to get jobs from Tom.

"That's it," Sally said. "It's all over."

"He won?"

"After he dumps Clyde in the river."

"When do they do that?"

"They'll take a break now."

Clint looked over at the judges. The two men were there, but he didn't see Marguerite.

"I'll be back before they start," he told Sally.

"Where are you goin'?"

"Just to check something."

***

Clint circled around behind where the judges were standing, kept to the trees so nobody would see him. As he watched he saw Marguerite moving in among some other trees, where nobody would be able to see her.

She paced, her arms crossed beneath her breasts. It was obvious she was waiting for someone. Finally, that someone appeared.

Clyde Norton.

Still wet from the river, he moved in among the same trees and joined her. They started to talk and then the talk became heated. He grabbed her by the arms, and she pulled away. They exchanged more words, then suddenly he was talking and she was listening. He stuck his index finger in her face and kept wagging it while he talked. She stood stiffly and did not respond. Finally he stopped talking and seemed to be waiting for a response. When she nodded her head once, he turned and walked away.

Clint had the feeling he'd just seen a deal happening.

FORTY-TWO

"**W**here were you?" Sally asked, when he came back. "They're about to start."

"I just had something to do."

"Well, watch this."

He did. He watched while the two men balanced on opposite sides of the log. He watched as they started to move their feet, spinning the log, and he watched as—in very quick time—Clyde Norton went flying off into the water.

This time when Tom Allen threw his hands in the air, the whole hillside seemed to erupt into cheers.

"That's it!" Sally said. "He won!"

Clint kept watching as Tom walked along the log and got off on the river's edge.

"What's the matter?" Sally asked, prodding him. "Tom's the winner?"

"Don't the judges have to decide that?"

"Well, yeah," Sally said, "but he won most of the events. There's no way he can lose."

"Let's just wait for the judges to make the announcement."

"That happens back at the judges stand," she said. "Come on, we can meet Tom and Luke there."

"Where has Luke been all this time?"

"Watching from somewhere else," she said. "Come on!"

***

They got back to where the judges stand was, along with a crowd of people, some of whom were spectators, the rest competitors. Clint looked around, saw Luke about the same time the big man saw them and waved. Sally waved back and dragged Clint over.

"He won!" she said. "Tom won!"

"It looks like it," Luke said. "What do you think, Clint?"

"I wasn't here for the whole day," Clint admitted, "but I think we'll have to wait for the judges' announcement."

"That's crazy," Sally insisted. "He won."

At that point, Tom himself came walking over. Sally hugged him and Luke slapped him on the back.

"Do you think you won?" Clint asked.

"Seems like it to me," Tom said, "but let's see what the judges have to say."

Clint looked at the crowd of people gathered around the judge's stand again and was surprised—although why should he be?—to see Harry Boyce. Of course, Boyce would be wanting to see who he'd be doing business with. It didn't look like he had any ranch hands with him, or that he had replaced his gunman, Frank Titleman, since firing him.

The judges were huddled on their stand, conversing intensely. In fact, they looked to Clint like they were arguing.

"What's takin' so long?" Sally said. "It's obvious."

"I don't like this," Luke said. "Marguerite is really arguin'."

"I can see that," Tom said.

Clint remained silent. He'd had a bad feeling ever since he saw Marguerite and Clyde arguing.

Finally, the judges stepped apart, and Marguerite moved forward. Behind her the two male judges continued to have a conversation between them.

"All right," Marguerite said, "we have the winner."

Impatient people moved closer to the judge's stand. Clint, Sally, Tom and Luke remained where they were.

"The winner of the Harold Boyce Lumber Contract is... Clyde Norton!"

FORTY-THREE

The noise in Blackie's Saloon was loud. Clint, Tom, Luke and Sally were holding down one end of the bar.

"This ain't right!" Sally shouted. "Nobody thinks it's right."

"Take it easy, Sally," Tom said.

"She's right," Luke said. "The boys in here ain't happy."

"The boys in here are gonna get work," Tom said. "By mornin' that's all they'll care about."

"He's right," Clint said.

"See?" Tom said.

"What?" Sally said, looking at Clint.

"But I agree with them," Clint said to Tom. "This isn't right."

"Clyde won," Tom said.

"I'm not so sure."

"What's that mean?"

"Before the last event, I saw Clyde and Marguerite in the forest," Clint said.

"Were they ruttin'?" Sally asked.

"No they were talking."

"About what?" Luke asked.

"They were arguing, really," Clint said. "And then Marguerite got quiet and Clyde gave her a real talking to,

189

with finger pointing and everything."

"Then he was tellin' her somethin'," Tom said.

"Right."

"Like maybe... she better fix it so he wins?" Tom asked.

"That's what I'm thinking."

"Sonofabitch!" Sally swore. "I'm gonna tear that bitch's tits off!"

"We don't have to go that far," Tom said. "We just have to get her to admit she did it."

"And how do we do that?" Luke asked.

"Maybe we don't," Clint said.

"Whataya mean?" Sally asked.

"Well, you told me Marguerite is cold," Clint said, "and I kind of found that out myself. I don't know that she'd talk to us."

"So what do you suggest?" Tom asked.

"The other two judges," Clint said. "The three of them were arguing intensely on the stand. We need to talk to those two and get them to admit that she fixed the results."

Tom looked around the saloon.

"I don't see Clyde in here," he said. "You'd think he'd be here celebratin'."

"Maybe," Luke said, "he's with Boyce at the other saloon, celebratin'."

"Luke," Clint said, "you go and see if Clyde's at the cattleman's saloon with Boyce."

"And what are you gonna do?"

"Tom and I are going to go and talk to the judges."

"What about me?" Sally asked. "You want me to go and talk to that bitch, Marguerite?"

"No," Clint said, "I don't want you to be tempted to rip her tits off."

"It would be my pleasure."

"No," Clint said, "you wait here for us."

"I could help with the judges."

"How so?" Clint asked. "They probably won't talk in front of you."

"You don't think so?" She had a sly smile on her face.

"What are you getting at?" Tom asked.

"You can't see it?" she asked.

"See what?"

"Those two men," she said, "they're afraid of women. They're afraid of Marguerite."

Clint looked at Tom. "She may have a point."

"So what do we do?" Tom asked.

"Let's take her with us," Clint said, then looked at Sally, "but you wait in the hall until we call for you."

"Okay," she said, "you got a deal. Let's go."

"And me?" Luke asked.

"You still go check the other saloon," Clint said. "We'll all meet back here in about an hour. It shouldn't take much longer than that." He looked at Tom. "We're going to straighten this out.

FORTY-FOUR

"**O**kay," Clint said to Sally, outside of the judge's hotel rooms, "you wait out here."

"But I can help—"

"I know you can," Clint said. "First, we've got to get them into the same room. Stay here on the stairway until you see us get them into one room, and then come and wait outside the door. Okay?"

"Okay," she agreed.

"Come on," he said to Tom.

Clint went to the first judge's door, and Tom went to the second.

"Mr. Strong," Clint said, "do you mind if we come in?"

"We? Who else—"

Tom came from down the hall with the other judge, Tompkins.

"The three of us," Clint said. "We'd like to come in and have a talk."

"About what?"

"We can talk about that inside," Clint sad. He stepped aside and Tom shoved the pear-shaped judge Tompkins into the room. He and Clint stepped in and closed the door, turned to face the two men.

"What's the meaning of this?" Strong asked, his voice tremulous.

"You tell us," Clint said. "What happened at that competition today? How could you allow Marguerite to announce Clyde Norton as the winner?"

"Well—she, uh, she—" Tompkins started.

"She's the head judge," Tompkins said. "It's her job."

"It's your job to judge fairly," Clint said. "The outcome was not a fair one. Everyone who was there knows that Tom Allen was the winner."

"It—it's the judge's decision as to who the winner is," Tompkins said.

"The three of you were arguing real good on that judges stand," Clint said. "What was the argument about?"

"It was just a discussion," Strong said. "Nothing more."

"We judged fairly," Tompkins insisted.

Clint knew they could probably beat the truth out of them, but that wasn't his style. It wasn't beyond Tom Allen, though. He knew that. But first they had another option to try.

He went to the door and opened it.

"Sally? Would you come in, please?"

Sally entered the room and glared at the two judges.

"W-what's she doing here?" Tompkins asked.

"Since you won't answer our questions," Clint said, "you're going to have to answer hers."

"Wha—what are you talking about?" Tompkins asked.

Clint and Tom started for the door.

"Where are you going?" Strong said. "You can't leave us in here with her. It ain't right."

"Oh, come on, fellas," she said, starting to unbutton her shirt. "We're just gonna have us some fun."

FORTY-FIVE

When the door to the room opened ten minutes later, Sally stepped out, buttoning her shirt.

"I think they're ready to talk to you now."

"What did you do?" Tom asked.

"I just showed them what a real woman looks like," she said. "They were so afraid of Marguerite, but now they're afraid of me."

"Why were they afraid of her?" Tom asked.

"Well," Sally said, "for one thing she's a woman, and I told you about that. Also, when she was made head judge, she chose them to sit on either side of her. She knew they'd vote any way she told them to."

Clint and Tom reentered the room, with Sally behind them. The two men were sitting on the bed with their hands in their lap, like they were hiding something.

"What was the argument on the judge's stand about?" Clint asked, getting right to the point.

"Marguerite wanted Clyde Norton to win," Tompkins said, "but it was obvious from the points that Mr. Allen, here, was the winner."

"Then why was Clyde Norton announced as the winner?" Tom asked.

"Well..." Tompkins said.

"Marguerite is a very forceful woman," Strong said, his eyes watery, "very forceful."

"So Marguerite arranged with Clyde Norton for him to win," Clint said.

"She did," Tompkins said.

"She knew that the competition would come down to Mr. Allen and Mr. Norton," Strong said. "That it would be a close contest, and she'd be safe giving it to Mr. Norton."

"But it wasn't that close, was it?" Sally asked.

"N-no," Tompkins said, flinching when Sally spoke to him, " Mr. Allen actually won by quite a convincing margin."

"She thinks she can get away with this?" Sally demanded. She looked at Clint. "We gotta go to her room and tell 'er she can't."

"I think I agree with Sally, Clint," Tom said. "We can't let her get away with this."

"I agree," Clint said. "But first," he looked at the two men, "how involved was Harry Boyce in this?"

"As far as we know, he wasn't," Tompkins said.

"We never heard anything about him being involved before," Strong said.

"Why would he be?" Tom asked. "If he wanted to give the job to Clyde he could have just given it to him. He didn't have to arrange for the competition to decide who he'd hire."

"I guess you're right," Clint said. He looked at the two judges again. "What about Ed Fenner?"

"Who?" Tompkins asked. He was eyeing Sally. Although he seemed afraid of her, he also seemed fascinated by her. Clint wondered just how much she had shown them.

"The gandy dancer who was killed," Clint said. "Fenner. You know anything about that?"

The two judges exchanged a glance, kept their hands

folded in their lap.

"Come on!" Clint demanded.

"We don't know who killed him," Tompkins said.

"But we think Marguerite does," Strong said.

"Why do you think that?"

"We wondered about the killing," Tompkins said, "but Marguerite told us not to worry about it."

"She just seemed to be... informed," Strong said, with a shrug.

"All right," Clint said, He looked at Tom and Sally. "I think I should talk to Marguerite alone."

"And then?" Sally asked.

"If she gives me the killer," he said, "we'll go and get him. And then we'll inform Mr. Boyce that the contest was fixed, and Tom actually won."

"Why would he believe you?" Sally asked.

"Because I'll get Clyde Norton to admit it," Clint said. "Tom's going to get that contract."

"Suits me," Tom said. "Go ahead. We'll wait here with these two and make sure they don't go anywhere."

"We didn't do anything," Tompkins complained.

"Shut up!" Sally snapped, and both men flinched as Clint went out the door.

FORTY-SIX

Clint walked to the end of the hall and knocked on the door of Marguerite's suite.

"I was hoping it would be you," she said, with a smile. She had already changed into something comfortable. "I think I need another treatment."

She turned and walked away from the door, leaving it open for him.

"Wine?" she asked, as he entered.

"No," he said, "I didn't come here for wine, Marguerite, or to go to bed with you."

"Really?" she asked, facing him. "Then why are you here? I really can't im—"

"You fixed the competition for Clyde Norton to win," Clint said. "You're going to change the results."

"I don't know whether to say 'did I?' or 'am I?' first."

"You did and you are," Clint said. "I saw you in the wood with Norton before the last event."

Her smile slipped for just a second, and then she said, "That had nothing to do with—"

"And I just came from a conversation with your two fellow judges," he added, cutting her off. "They talked."

She stared at him.

"The decision is not going to stand, Marguerite," he said. "You and me, we're going to go and talk to Mr. Boyce right now."

"What makes you think I'd do that?"

"If you don't come with me," he said. "Sally Hayfield is down the hall and she's just itching for an excuse to rip your tits off. Should I go and get her?"

Marguerite blanched.

"That sow!"

"Wait," he said, reaching for the door, "I'll go and get her so you can say that to her face."

"No!"

"Are you coming?"

"Look," she said, "Clyde Norton forced me—"

"More like he paid you off."

"All right yes, he paid me, but he forced me to take the money," she said. "You don't know the kind of man he is."

"Well, he's probably over at the saloon with Boyce," Clint said. "Let's go and see what kind of men they both are."

"He'll kill me, Clint!" she said, appearing frightened for the first time. "Like he killed Ed Fenner."

"How do you know he killed Fenner?"

"Clyde and I were talking in the alley next to the saloon," she said, "and we didn't know Fenner was further inside the alley. He was lying there, drunk, but he heard us—he knew Clyde wanted me to fix the results."

"So Clyde just happened to have an axe with him, and killed Fenner?" Clint asked.

"Clyde told me to go to my hotel, and said he'd take care of Fenner."

"All right, Marguerite," he said, "come on. I'm not going to let anything happen to you—unless you don't cooperate with me. Then I'll put you in a room alone with Sally."

"You wouldn't!"

"Try me."

"Let me get my wrap." She walked to a chair where the wrap was lying, reached for it, and came up with a small derringer just as Clint crossed the room and reached her. He grabbed her wrist and yanked her arm as she pulled the trigger, firing one shot into the ceiling.

"Why do I have the feeling you're not the innocent you claim to be in all this?" he asked, taking the derringer away.

"There's no law here!" she said. "You can't do this."

"There's lumberjack law here, and I'm the one who's going to enforce it!"

FORTY-SEVEN

Clint marched down the street, dragging Marguerite by the wrist, while Tom and Sally followed.

"Sally," Clint said, "go to Blackie's and get Luke. He won't want to miss this."

"Okay." She ran across the street.

"That woman—" Marguerite started, but Clint cut her off.

"—is more woman than you'll ever be!"

"Oh, please," she said.

Clint stopped, jerking her to a stop by her wrist. Tom stopped with them.

"There's no reason you should be so high and mighty now, Marguerite!"

She fell silent.

When they got to the cattleman's saloon Clint noticed a sign had been put up over the doors. It said BOYCE'S SALOON. Apparently, this would satisfy Harry Boyce until he could get the whole town named after him.

Clint looked over the batwing doors, saw that the saloon was filled with cowhands, a few guns in among them. Further examination showed Harry Boyce seated at a back table, drinking with Clyde Norton.

Marguerite tried to pull away from him, but he said, "Let's go inside and get this over with."

He pulled her through the doors with him, Tom Allen

following behind them. It instantly became quiet, and they became the center of attention.

"Well," Boyce said, loudly, "Mr. Adams, are you here to celebrate Mr. Norton's victory with us?"

"Not exactly," Clint said. "I'm actually here to celebrate Tom Allen's victory."

"What are you talkin' about?" Clyde Norton demanded. He stood up. "I won that contest fair and square."

"Why would you put it that way, Norton?" Clint asked. "Did you think I was going to accuse you of cheating?"

"Cheatin'?" Norton looked around, uncomfortably. "Well, no, of course not."

"Well, I am," Clint said. He looked at Harry Boyce, who was still seated, a cigar in one hand, a glass of whiskey in the other. "Norton conspired with the head judge here, and fixed the results."

A murmur went up in the room, but the cowhands had no chips in this game. They didn't care who cut their boss's trees, Tom or Clyde. They were just interested in the action in the room.

"What are you talking about?" Boyce asked.

At that moment Sally and Luke entered the saloon, saw that things had progressed, so they stepped aside to watch.

"Norton forced Marguerite, here, to fix the results so he'd get the contract," Clint explained. "Most of the onlookers and competitors agree that Tom won by a long way."

"Miss Montero?" Boyce said, standing. He put his glass down, but kept hold of his cigar. "Do you have something to say?"

Clint pushed Marguerite in front of him and finally released her wrist.

She looked at Norton, who glowered at her.

"Well..." she said.

"Come on," Boyce said. "Out with it."

"I can bring the other two judges in here," Clint offered. "They'll tell you."

"That's not necessary," Boyce said. "Miss Montero looks like she has something to say."

"I—I—" she stammered. "It's true. Clyde Norton forced me to fix the results."

"You bitch!" Norton said. He turned to Boyce. "She came to me with the plan, said she'd fix it if I paid her!"

"And you took her up on her offer," Boyce said.

"I—I wanted that contract," Norton said. "So... yes, I did."

Boyce stared at Norton, then shook his head and shifted his gaze to Clint and Tom.

"I planned this competition because I wanted to be sure I got the right man for the job," he said. "Mr. Allen, it appears that would be you."

"Thank you, sir."

Boyce looked at Norton.

"I assume you'll be leaving town," he said, "and you can take Miss Montero with you."

"Yeah, okay," Norton said.

"Actually," Clint said, "that's not the plan."

FORTY-EIGHT

"What are you talking about?" Harry Boyce asked. "What else is there?"

"Well," Clint said, "there's the question of Ed Fenner's murder."

"What's that got to do with this?" the rancher asked.

Clint reached for Marguerite and eased her back behind him.

"I believe Clyde Norton may have killed him," he said, "and if he didn't do it himself, he knows who did."

"What?" Clyde barked. "That's ridiculous."

Clint turned to Marguerite.

The undertaker told me you went over there to see Ed's body," he said.

"Um, that's right—"

"Why?"

She licked her lips. "Clyde told me to go."

"Why?"

"He wanted to know if the undertaker knew anything about who'd killed him."

"He wanted you to ask him?"

"There were other men there," she said, "friends of Fenner's. he just wanted me to listen."

Boyce turned to Norton.

"Why would you do that?"

Norton's eyes began to dart around the room, but

there was no help for him. These were all cowhands who were just spectators.

He made a dash for the door. None of the cowhands made a move to stop him. It was up to Clint, who stepped in front of the bull of a man. But before Norton could slam into him, Clint was pushed aside by Luke, who took the brunt of Norton's rush. The two men went crashing to the floor, and it was Luke who rolled on top of Norton and held him down.

"Sorry," Luke said, looking up at Clint, "but I knew he'd knock you though a window."

"Thanks, Luke." Clint leaned down to speak to Norton. "Is there anybody else you want to take down with you, Clyde?"

"Just that bitch!" he spat. "The fix was her idea."

"And the murder?" Clint asked. "She have anything to do with it?"

"She knew about it!"

"But I—I didn't have anything to do with the actual killing," she said. She looked around with pleading eyes, focusing on Harry Boyce. "I—there was nothing I could do to stop him."

"Of course not, Madam," Boyce said. He walked to her and took her hand. "Why don't you come and sit with me, have a drink while they take care of Mr. Norton."

"Oh, why, thank you, Mr. Boyce... thank you very much."

Clint watched as Boyce walked her to his table and sat her down. He actually believed that she had assisted in the murder, but it was up to Boyce if he wanted to forgive her for the fix.

"Mr. Allen," Boyce said, "would you like to celebrate your victory?"

"If you don't mind, Mr. Boyce, I'll do that with my

men over at Blackie's."

"I don't mind at all," Boyce said. "Let's get together tomorrow to discuss the terms of our contract."

"That's fine with me."

Tom reached down and helped Luke get Norton to his feet, and they walked him outside, with Clint and Sally behind them.

"Where can we put him until I can take him to the law in Cascade?" Clint asked.

"When do you plan to do that?" Tom asked.

"Tomorrow," Clint said. "There's no point in waiting. The games are over, right?"

"That's right," Tom said. "Now the business starts."

"And I don't have any interest in the lumber business."

"Well, we can lock him in a room over at the club."

"Okay," Clint said. "Do that and I'll pick him up in the morning."

"Right."

"And you'll have to have somebody keep an eye out, make sure he doesn't escape."

"We'll put some men on it," Luke assured him.

Together, they walked Clyde Norton down the street to the Lumberjack Club.

"You sure you want to leave tomorrow?" Sally asked.

"Yep," he said. "I've had enough to this no-name town."

"Well then," she said, grabbing his hand, "let's go over to the hotel. I wanna show you that all the games ain't quite done, after all."

He let her pull him along, not bothering to tell her that Dave Cabrera was still on the bed in his room.

ABOUT THE AUTHOR

As "J.R. Roberts" Bob Randisi is the creator and author of the long running western series, *The Gunsmith*. Under various other pseudonyms he has created and written the "Tracker," "Mountain Jack Pike," "Angel Eyes," "Ryder," "Talbot Roper," "The Son of Daniel Shaye," and "the Gamblers" Western series. His western short story collection, *The Cast-Iron Star and Other Western Stories*, is now available in print and as an ebook from Western Fictioneers Books.

In the mystery genre he is the author of the *Miles Jacoby, Nick Delvecchio, Gil & Claire Hunt, Dennis McQueen, Joe Keough,* and *The Rat Pack,* series. He has written more than 500 western novels and has worked in the Western, Mystery, Sci-Fi, Horror and Spy genres. He is the editor of over 30 anthologies. All told he is the author of over 650 novels. His arms are very, very tired.

He is the founder of the Private Eye Writers of America, the creator of the Shamus Award, the co-founder of Mystery Scene Magazine, the American Crime Writers League, Western Fictioneers and their Peacemaker Award.

In 2009 the Private Eye Writers of America awarded him the Life Achievement Award, and in 2013 the Readwest Foundation presented him with their President's Award for Life Achievement.

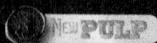